Secrets of a Baby Mama 2
by

D T Pollard

Essence Bestselling Author
Based upon Ratchet Woman 2 by D T Pollard

2

1

Tameka's husband Terrance walked into the bedroom after getting home from work and was met with an unexpected and confusing sight.

"Tameka! Why are all of these suitcases sitting here open on top of the bed?" Terrance Henderson said to his wife of one year.

"They're on the bed so you can pack all of your shit in them and get the fuck out of my house!" Tameka answered back angrily.

"What the hell are you talking about? Why would I need to pack my stuff up and leave?" Terrance said as he followed his wife into the living room.

"Oh, so you're going to try and play dumb with me. I'll tell you why. When you were taking a shower last night a text message came on your phone and I read it. It was from that hoe I went to high school with, Keisha Brooks. It said meet me at mama's house at noon tomorrow," Tameka said.

"Look baby I can't stop somebody from sending me a text," Terrance said.

"Terrance, why would that nasty bitch even have your phone number in the first place?! Answer that shit?! You must think I'm a fool!" Tameka said.

"Look Tameka, baby you got this all twisted," Terrance said.

"I got it twisted, huh. I played it off and didn't say anything. I even gave you some last night when you wanted it so you wouldn't suspect anything. Let me tell you something Terrance. I took a personal day off and went over to that bitch's mother's house at twelve thirty today. I saw the county car that you drive at work parked behind her house. I walked up on the porch. The dumb hoe needs to learn to close the curtains all the way. All I could see was her big ass moving back and forth on the sofa with your skinny legs sticking out from under that fat ass. I recognized the tattoo on your leg, so you need to pack your shit and leave now!" Tameka said.

Terrance just stood there.

"Why should I leave?" Terrance asked.

"Nigga, this is my house! You moved in with me and my kids after we got married. Your name's not on the mortgage here. You can take your ass over to Keisha's house, oh, I forgot, Keisha doesn't have a house, she's living with her mother. While her mother is at work, she's over there hoeing it up, living off food stamps and your dumb ass just fell in there behind the rest of those sorry ass niggas she's been fucking. Terrance, we're married. You said you loved me and would be a father to my kids and then you did this to me. Were you lying and just pretending? I don't understand this Terrance!" Tameka said.

"Tameka, I don't know what to say. Everything was great before we got married. We used to have fun together. Now with three kids and work, it's not the same," Terrance said.

"What? Is that what it is? As long as it was just fun, everything was fine. When mama kept my kids while we went out, everything was fine. When I was coming over to your apartment before we got

4

married and fucking you, everything was fine. It was only after we got married and real life set it, then it's wasn't fun anymore. Guess what, you knew I had three children when we met. Did you think they were just going to disappear when we got married or did you think I would handle the kids on my own since they were mine and you could do whatever the fuck you pleased? That's some weak ass bullshit. It's called a marriage Terrance. It's not a video game. Both people have to put in work. So, are you telling me you went and fucked that nasty heifer because you weren't having fun anymore? All that tells me is you can't handle responsibility and that's not a being a man, that's being a weak ass nigga like the rest of them I've dealt with for years. I'm tired and you just need to pack up and go!" Tameka said.

"Alright, so it's like that! I'll tell you how I see it. Yeah, I thought I loved you until we got married, then it was like you wanted to control my life. I'm running your kids all over the place. Picking them up from one thing or another, school, day care or something else, I felt like I was in prison. I couldn't hang out with my boys anymore and we didn't do the things we used to do before we got married. I ran into Keisha and she hollered at a nigga and said she wouldn't sweat me like that. I've been fucking her for three months now. The only reason I hadn't left already is because I didn't want to mess up a good thing here. You treat me pretty good, this is a nice house and as long as I threw you a little dick every once in a while, you were cool. You're trying to call Keisha a hoe, she called you a run through baby mama. Keisha doesn't have three kids by different baby daddies like you. My boys all said I was a fool to even marry you with three children already by different men in the first place. A skank hoe letting every nigga out there have his turn, then after that pussy was tapped out you want to play like a wifey and get married. I was just the dumb motherfucka that fell for it!" Terrance said.

"What did you just say to me? If that's what you thought why did you marry me in the first place?" Tameka asked.

"Well, you know what they say about trying to turn a hoe into a housewife," Terrance remarked.

"What! You are the one cheating on me! That's it! Just get the fuck out!" Tameka said in a fit of rage with tears streaming down her cheeks as she jumped up into Terrance's face.

Terrance stepped back and drew his arm back in a motion like he was about to strike Tameka with the back of his right hand before he realized what he was doing. Tameka was stunned that this man that stood before God and pledged his love to her one year earlier had raised his hand in anger to her. Tameka stepped back in shock at Terrance's actions.

"What! Were you going to hit me? You hate me that much? You better go ahead and do it because I've got something for your ass!" Tameka said crying.

"Tameka, I'm sorry baby. I didn't mean to raise my hand to you," Terrance said.

Tameka walked back to the bedroom and in less than a minute she came back into the living room. "Tameka! What the hell are you doing with that gun?" Terrance asked. "You didn't know I had this did you. I never thought I would have to pull it on my own husband. I never even had a gun until some guy tried to rape my friend Lindsay. A woman she worked with saw her car parked on side of the road and stopped. That woman had a gun and made the guy let her go. I decided it would be a good idea for me to learn how to use a gun since I was a single woman with three little kids. The last person I thought I would need to pull it on to protect myself was you," Tameka said as she pointed the gun at Terrance.

"Tameka, calm down. You don't want to accidently pull the trigger on that thing," Terrance said.

"Motherfucka, if I pull the trigger it won't be an accident. I took a course on how to use this gun and have a right to carry permit. You better leave before you make me do something to you I can't undo. You just don't know how pissed off I am right now. After all I did for you. You called me a hoe and pulled your hand back to hit me. I even bought you a car for your birthday. Just leave and I'll send your shit to you later!" Tameka said.

"Okay, I'll go, but you'll regret this. With three kids, ain't no other man going to be looking at you for nothing but a quick fuck as a side hoe," Terrance said.

7

"I'd rather be by myself than be with a man that doesn't respect me or himself. Why are you messing with an uneducated hoe like Keisha when you have a wife at home with a good job and a college education? Maybe that was the problem, I wasn't easy to impress so you had to get with somebody you thought you could run your bullshit game on. You just watch, when you're out of here, she won't have anything to do with you. Women like her only want somebody else's man because it makes them feel powerful to think a man would risk destroying his home life to be with them. When you are free and clear, you're no good to her anymore, she gets her rocks off by thinking she's getting over on me, not from being with you, you're just too dumb to see that and one other thing Terrance. The only reason that hoe Keisha doesn't have a house full of kids is because the bitch keeps getting abortions. She likes to sleep with married men and having a baby by another woman's husband is one of the quickest ways to end up dead," Tameka said.

"Tameka I'm leaving. You can send my stuff over to mama's house. I guess you'll be filing for a divorce," Terrance said.

"You damn right I'm filing for a divorce and taking my maiden name back. I made it this far by being Tameka Davis so I'm sure not going to through the rest of my life wearing your sorry ass last name," Tameka said as Terrance left.

Tameka locked the door and sat down on the sofa while shaking. She placed her gun on the coffee table, put her hands to her forehead and cried like a baby. The way the man she loved treated her left Tameka with even deeper wounds and distrust of men than she had before. This was the loneliest Tameka had felt in years. Tameka purposely left her children over at her parent's house because she knew this confrontation with Terrance was coming up when he got home and she didn't want them around to witness what could happen.

Tameka picked up her cell phone and pressed a stored number.

"Lindsay, I just threw Terrance out," Tameka said to her oldest friend.

Lindsay Jefferson was Tameka's oldest and closest friend. Tameka and Lindsay had walked through life and relationship hell together for years as they struggled in Dallas to raise their children alone without their fathers while leaning on each other. Tameka thought they had both finally found happiness in their lives and relationships when Lindsay married the father of her oldest son, ex-professional football player RJ Jefferson and about one year later Tameka married a man she thought was the love of her life, Terrance Henderson, but that had just gone up in flames. Tameka thought of all of the long nights walking the concrete floors of that massive big box discount store she used to work at when she was in Dallas to put food on the table.

Tameka would go to work after Lindsay came in from a long night dancing at the strip club so one of them could be at home with their five children. Given her luck with men, Tameka felt cursed at relationships and even thought back on the time she knowingly served as a side chick for a married lawyer because he was helping her close the gap in paying bills that her paycheck didn't quite cover. That life ended when her good friend Lindsay blessed her with $250,000 dollars after she got her settlement from RJ Jefferson because of the circumstances of how he fathered Lindsay's son. Tameka didn't squander her good fortune and moved back home, earned her college degree and got a good job. Tameka thought her life was perfect until she saw that text message on her husband's cell phone. "Lindsay, I thought he was going to hit me. He drew his hand back at me. I got so mad that I went and got my gun and told him to leave. I'm just shaking over this," Tameka said sobbing.

"You had to pull a gun on him, oh my God! Tameka, I'm so sorry. I didn't think Terrance would do something like that, are you going to be okay?" Lindsay asked.

"Yeah, I'll be okay. I've got to explain to my kids that Terrance is gone. They had even started calling him daddy. Oh my God Lindsay, that's why over all those years I stopped myself from bringing different men around my kids and then I got married and look at what happened. What the hell was wrong with him if he thought marriage was some kind of amusement park? We still had fun and he wasn't missing anything in the sex department, I made sure of that. I guess he just liked to get in the gutter with that slut he was messing with," Tameka said.

"Tameka you need a break. Why don't you take some time off and come chill out with me for a while. You and the kids can stay in the guest house. Our children haven't seen each other in a while and it'll take their mind off Terrance being gone," Lindsay said.

"That's sounds like a good idea. I have a couple weeks of vacation and the kids are out of school. Don't you have to ask RJ first?" Tameka said.

"Ask RJ, please? If I say you can come, then you can come. I've got RJ's ass under control," Lindsay said.

"Bitch, you still crazy. One day that white chocolate trap is gonna stop working," Tameka said laughing.

"That'll be when I'm in my wheelchair. I'll have to hold on to the handle to twerk then," Lindsay said.

"Oh my God, you're so silly," Tameka said.

"See, I got you laughing, didn't I? Call me when you work your schedule out. Love you Tameka. It will be okay," Lindsay said.

"Love you too Lindsay," Tameka said as she hung up the phone.

Tameka sat back and smiled before she got up to drive over to her parents to pick up her three children and she knew Lindsay was right, things would be okay again, but at that moment she was emotionally cut to the bone. Tameka informed her parents of what happened between her and Terrance. Tameka's parents told her not to worry and they would help her with the children. Tameka's father told Tameka that a real man would come along who would appreciate the woman she was now and love her children.

The next day Tameka packed up Terrance's clothes and other effects and sent them over to his mother's house. A visit to a lawyer was Tameka's next course of action and Terrance put up no resistance. Just as Tameka predicted, Keisha didn't want anything to do with Terrance after he was thrown out of the house. Keisha just tallied up

12

Tameka's broken marriage to her growing total of failed relationships she had caused over the years.

As Tameka was leaving her lawyers office she spotted Keisha Brooks coming out of a convenience store farther down the sidewalk with two bags in her hand. Tameka was walking to her car when she heard a call to her.

"Hey Tameka, how're you doing," Keisha said.

Tameka froze in her tracks and tried to compose herself.

"What, you can't speak?" Keisha asked.

To Keisha's surprise, Tameka turned and walked up to her. Tameka was about three inches taller than Keisha and stood right in front of her with her hands on her hips.

"Hoe, you got the nerve to say something to me with your stank ass. Don't get it twisted. I've known you for a long time, but we're grown women now. This ain't high school anymore. Don't mess around and get fucked up, because one day you gonna fuck the wrong woman's man and your ass is going six feet under. You're just not worth it to me, or else I could have dropped your ass with my 9 while he was fucking you in your mama's house. I sure couldn't miss that big ass of yours. Don't say shit to me anymore hoe, you got that," Tameka said as she walked away with a smile on her face.

Keisha stood there shaken by what Tameka had just said to her. Keisha thought she was making light of the fact that she had broken up another marriage, but she didn't expect the comeback she got from a woman scorned. Keisha quickly got in her mother's car and drove off.

Tameka took Lindsay up on her offer and two weeks later she drove up to Oklahoma City with her three children Joquan, Malik and Tasha. Joquan was nine years old. Malik was seven and Tasha was five. The upcoming school year would be the first in which all of Tameka's children would be attending school with Tasha entering kindergarten. In a way this marked a milestone for Tameka because now if she took a day off from work she would actually have some time to herself and being single again meant that those times would be in short supply.

As Tameka drove past the gate to get to Lindsay's massive home she shared with RJ, she thought back on the apartments they shared for years with five children and two adult women crammed together in order to survive. Tameka rang the doorbell and within a minute the door opened with screams.

"Tameka!" Lindsay screamed as she hugged her friend.

"Lindsay!" Tameka said as she hugged her back.

The kids ran into the house and immediately began to breakout into rooms where toys and video games were located.

"Hey Tameka, it's good to see you," RJ said as he came downstairs.

"It's good to see you to. You're holding up pretty good for your age. You're over thirty now aren't you?" Tameka said jokingly.

"Oh, you got jokes. Yes, I'm over thirty now, but I feel pretty good. Hey, I'm sorry. I heard about what happened with Terrance, I didn't think he was that kind of guy. I'm shocked, actually," RJ said.

"I guess you don't really know someone until they get under pressure. You know dating and all that is not like being married with real responsibilities. It's after that day to day grind sets in that brings out what somebody is really all about. Just look at how sweet Lindsay was until you put that ring on her finger," Tameka said.

"Bitch, no you didn't. I'm always a sweetheart, aren't I RJ?" Lindsay said.

"Well on that note, I'm going to leave you two ladies alone," RJ said as he walked away.

"RJ you didn't answer. You'll want something pretty soon," Lindsay said to RJ as he left the room.

"Lindsay, I was downtown coming out of the lawyer's office and guess who was coming out of a store right down the sidewalk from me, Keisha? I tried to be civilized and ignored the heifer, and then she had the nerve to say something to me. The bitch said 'Hi Tameka' and then got smart and asked if I was going to speak to her. She better be glad that I'm saved now, because back in the day I would have dragged her fat ass right there on that sidewalk. What kind of hoe has the nerve to say something to me after knowing that I knew she had fucked my husband? That's just a low down ratchet attitude," Tameka said.

15

"Well you know Keisha was a young hoe in training in high school. I heard she was even fucking one of the coaches. You can't blame her if she's a natural born slut there's not much you can do about that. Now Terrance, that's a different story, he's the one who said those wedding vows to you, not Keisha. Terrance promised to not let anyone come between you two and what did he do, he put his dick inside that nasty bitch when he had a loving wife at home. That's why I always said it makes no sense when people fight other folks when somebody cheats on them. The problem is with the person that made the promise to them, not the person they cheated with. I could leave this house right now and find a guy to fuck me within an hour because there always someone out there willing to do it, but I won't do that because I love RJ. Immature, weak ass men and women shouldn't get married because they can't flip the switch to being responsible adults," Lindsay said.

"I guess you're right, but it would have felt a little better if he was fucking a bitch that at least looked better than I do. That short, fat ass Keisha looks about like what she is, a pig," Tameka said.

"What the hell! So now you're even more pissed because he cheated on you with a bitch that looked worse than you do. That's some crazy thinking there. If the bitch would have looked better than you did, maybe you would feel better?" Lindsay said.

"Lindsay, don't front. I know you. If RJ was tipping on you with some woman and she turned out to be some snaggletoothed skank, you'd be more pissed than if she was a beauty queen," Tameka said.

"I'd be pissed that he stepped out on me, but not about how the woman looked. When you look as good as I do, anybody he gets with is going to look ugly by comparison anyway," Lindsay said.

"Lindsay, you are so full of shit," Tameka said.

"Come on and let me show you the guest house where you will be staying. We had it redecorated not too long ago, plus we can really talk in private there," Lindsay said.

3

Lindsay and Tameka walked into the guest house. Lindsay gave Tameka a tour of the three-bedroom home and then they took a seat side by side on the sofa in the living room.

"Lindsay, this guest house is bigger than your house in Dallas," Tameka commented.

"Yeah it is. We are so blessed to be in the position we're in now, but let's talk about you. Tell me everything that happened. Someone once told me it's good to unburden yourself, so give that weight to me," Lindsay offered.

"Well, everything started off great between us after we got married. Terrance was working and seemed to be very responsible. We were getting along great. I thought we were fine as a couple and I was crazy about him. I keep trying to figure out what went wrong," Tameka said.

"I know. Did he give you any clues?" Lindsay asked.

"You know my mother was keeping the kids a lot during the summer and I would pick them up on my way home from work. When school started things changed a little. I had to drive all the way to Tyler to work, so Terrance took the kids to school and mama picked them up when their day was over. Then when my boys had a program at school at night, Terrance would go, but wasn't very happy about it. He took the boys to get haircuts with him every Saturday. After a few months he started to complain that we never had any alone time anymore. He also started to hang out with his friends once a week for football night. I didn't think anything about it, but now that I can look back on it, I think he was pulling away form me. I thought our sex life was fine, but I was so tired that we only did it once or twice a week, but when we first got together, we were like rabbits and couldn't keep our hands off each other," Tameka said.

"So what was different in the beginning?" Lindsay asked.

"My children, when we first got together they weren't around most of the time. We always went out alone and when I visited him my mother always kept my kids when we were dating. After we got married things really changed after school started and I guess our real family life began," Tameka said.

"Tameka can't you see what happened?" Lindsay said.

"Terrance married you, but he didn't marry your family, because he didn't realized he was marrying four people instead of one," Lindsay said.

"I think you're right, because that's what he was talking about when I confronted him about Keisha. He said he felt trapped and was always driving my kids around for one thing or another," Tameka said.

"You see Tameka. Terrance told you out of his own mouth. You may have been too angry to hear him, but when he said he was driving your kids around and not that he was driving our kids around. Tameka, I don't know much about the bible, but I do listen when I go to church. The pastor talked about people being unequally yoked. I think he was talking about people that believe in God shouldn't be joined together with people that don't believe, but your marriage was like that too," Lindsay said.

"Lindsay, you're losing me," Tameka said.

"Okay, what I mean is when you got married, you both got married differently. Terrance married you, but you thought he was marrying you and your kids. It took him a while to realize that your children were real and came with you as a package deal, but it was too late. You didn't understand that your husband didn't want to be the head of a family of five until he told you to your face. Tameka, you were never really married to Terrance, at least not in the way you thought you were," Lindsay said.

"Lindsay, you're right, I set myself up for this by shielding Terrance from my children when we were dating. Why did I do that?" Tameka asked.

"I think you were trying to compensate for being a single mother with three kids by showing how great it was to be with you as a woman without kids. Terrance fell in love with you, made love to you and married you, but after you said I do, you went from a couple to a family of five. He wasn't ready for it," Lindsay said.

"Lindsay, the way you put it makes it seem like I tricked him into marrying me by hiding my children. He knew I had three children," Tameka said.

"No sweetie you tricked yourself. A man knowing you have three kids and experiencing what it means to be with a woman with three children are two different things. I know we always tried to keep from parading different men around our kids when we lived together, but when it starts to get as serious as you and Terrance were, then it's time to test drive that man as a potential leader of a family of five before you're standing at the altar," Lindsay said.

"You're right and I hate to admit it. I did over compensate for my children in the beginning. I hate to admit it, but deep down inside I feel like I have a handicap when comparing myself against a woman with no children. I love my kids to death, but why would a man choose me over a woman with no kids. Terrance said something to me that I said myself when we lived in Dallas. Do you remember that day when we went to the mall and were talking about our situations? I said I didn't just want to end up as some man's side chick, that's exactly what Terrance said I was good for with three children out of wedlock," Tameka said.

"He's wrong, but he wasn't the right man. Next time, and there will be a next time, don't try and hide that you're a baby mama, because those three children are going to show up at some point. The right man will love all of you and that includes your three children," Lindsay said.

"Do you really believe there's a man out there that can love all of us that much," Tameka said.

"Look we don't do like some of those women used to do back in the day if they had children before they got married. Some women would allow their children to live with relatives or let their parents raise them just so they could be

21

with a man. I knew of children left with their relatives while their mother moved far away with their new husband and started a new family. I always wondered how they felt about that. If RJ would not have married me unless I left Jasmine with her father's folks then it would have been deuces and I'll see your ass later," Lindsay said.

"I hear you Lindsay. I needed this talk. If another man says he wants to marry me, then he better get four rings because he's marrying all of us," Tameka said.

Tameka and Lindsay shared a big hug.

"I'm hungry. Let's go get something to eat," Lindsay said.

4

"Okay, we left RJ at home with five kids. Can he handle that? Tameka asked as she and Lindsay sat down for lunch at a restaurant located in the Bricktown Entertainment district in Oklahoma City,

"He'll be fine. He'll probably order some pizza and let them wear themselves out in the game room. What are you thinking?" Lindsay asked.

"I don't know Lindsay. I know we just had our talk, but I don't know if I can ever trust another man again. I feel like I'm done after this. What difference did marriage make, none? Is there something wrong with me or is it my judgment?" Tameka said.

"Tameka, why do you say that?" Lindsay asked.

"Look at my track record. One sorry ass guy after another, three kids by three different men and divorced after one year of marriage. I do think what we discussed with Terrance has some merit, but what am I doing wrong here?" Tameka asked.

"You're not doing anything wrong. We both made our share of mistakes when we were young, but Terrance was the one that screwed up, not you. You just haven't met the man that's worthy of you yet," Lindsay said.

"Well he needs to show up with a big sign over his head so I can tell him from all of the other clowns out there," Tameka said.

"There is a guy I know that asks about you every once in a while," Lindsay said.

"Who would you know that would ask about me?" Tameka said.

"Do you remember RJ's best man, Datron Jenkins?" Lindsay said.

"The big dude?" Tameka asked.

"Yeah, the big dude. For some reason you caught his eye at my wedding," Lindsay said.

"He might have said a couple of words to me, but that was it," Tameka said.

"I told him that you were in a relationship and he respected that and didn't want to cause any problems," Lindsay said.

"What does he ask about me?" Tameka asked.

"Datron's a little short on words, but he'll ask me how my tall, fine friend in Texas is doing," Lindsay said.

"So, I'm your tall fine friend in Texas. That's a trip. What about me got stuck in his head?" Tameka pondered.

"I know what got stuck in his head. Your butt got stuck in his head," Lindsay said.

"My butt, what?" Tameka said.

"I heard him tell RJ one day, that God built the perfect ass when he built yours, because of the way your dress was draped over it as you walked down the aisle. High and tight is how he described it. He said he liked your eyes and smile too," Lindsay said.

"I don't even know this man and he got all that from watching me walking down the aisle," Tameka said.

"Well at least you know you still got it," Lindsay said.

"Yeah, that, high, tight ass of mine got me three kids, that I love, and a lot of other baggage. I was young and stupid. I fell for every line. I want to marry you so we don't need to use protection, I want to feel the real you and if you really love me then show me with nothing between us. I was young and believed all of them. I didn't know some men could just lie to me like that to get what they wanted and then walk away. I can't even think about another man right now given where my head is," Tameka said.

Lindsay and Tameka drove back home. When they walked in, someone else was there.

"Datron, I didn't know you were coming by. How are you?" Lindsay said.

"I'm doing fine, how about you?" Datron said.

"I'm doing great. Datron, I don't know if you remember my friend Tameka from Texas? She was in our wedding," Lindsay said.

"Yeah, yeah, I think I remember you. It's nice to see you again," Datron said.

"I remember you being there. You were RJ's best man weren't you?" Tameka said.

"Yes, I served as my buddy's best man. He married a good woman. I was talking with your boys Joquan and Malik, they're some smart kids and your daughter too. They were calling me sir and a lot of children don't show respect like that today. You're raising some respectful kids," Datron said.

25

"Well, thank you. It was nice to see you again Datron," Tameka said as she and Lindsay walked down the hallway.

"Lindsay, is he looking at my butt?" Tameka asked,

Lindsay did a quick glance back and waved at Datron.

"Yes, he's looking at your butt," Lindsay said as they turned a corner and went into the living room.

"Did you notice what Datron did back there?" Lindsay asked.

"What do you mean?" Tameka asked.

"He complimented your kids. He let you know up front that he knew you had three children," Lindsay said.

"I guess you're right. Well he seems like a nice guy, but it's way too soon for me to be thinking about talking to a man, for God's sakes, I just got rid of one," Tameka said.

"Tameka nobody expects you to just jump out and marry some guy, but don't let what happened with Terrance make you miss out on a good man. If a man is really interested in you, he'll wait until you're ready," Lindsay said.

"I hear what you're saying. Let's go up front and talk with the guys," Tameka said.

Tameka and Lindsay joined RJ, Datron and the children up front. Tameka was surprised that she actually enjoyed Datron's conversation and found him to be an interesting guy.

"Tameka, I know you're just here for another week. I don't want to sound like I'm getting ahead of myself, but would you like to go to lunch or dinner?" Datron asked.

"Datron, I don't know. I recently filed for divorce from my husband. It feels awfully soon," Tameka said.

"I understand, but I just want to talk and shoot the breeze to get to know you before you leave. I know how it is when wounds are fresh. Right after my marriage broke up, I didn't want anything to do with anybody for a long time, but I finally realized that not every woman was like my ex-wife," Datron said.

Tameka paused in thought for a moment before answering.

"Okay, what can it hurt? I'll go to dinner with you, if Lindsay will watch my kids. We do have to eat, don't we?" Tameka said.

Tameka asked Lindsay if she would keep her children while she went out with Datron and Lindsay readily agreed. Datron told Tameka he would pick her up around seven on Friday night. Datron was a gentle giant of a man at six feet four inches tall and weighed two hundred and sixty pounds, but he had confined his furry to the football field until he retired one year earlier. Datron went with the shaved head look and was of a medium brown skin tone.

"Tameka, I think it's brave of you to go out with Datron. You need a change of pace," Lindsay said later.

"Maybe you're right. He seems like a nice guy. Well let me take these kids out to the guest house and get them in bed. Thank you for inviting us up here. It feels good to get away, plus I hadn't spent time with you in a long time," Tameka said.

Lindsay watched as Tameka and her children walked down the path to the guest house and it seemed like she could feel the emotional pain Tameka was enduring.

"Lindsay, how do I look?" Tameka asked as she spun around.

"Tameka, I've always said that next to me, you are the best looking woman I know. You look great. Now you're going out with a man tall enough that you can wear your six-inch heels and not be taller than he is," Lindsay said.

"Are you sure you didn't have anything to do with Datron being here when we got back the other day?" Tameka said.

"Don't look at me, but I can't speak for RJ," Lindsay said.

"Do you think he called him?" Tameka said.

"I ain't saying nothing," Lindsay said.

Datron arrived on Friday night to pick Tameka up for their date and came inside.

"Tameka you look great," Datron said.

"Thank you," Tameka said.

"Datron you behave yourself, this is my best friend you're taking out. Don't make me cut you off from those collard greens you like," Lindsay said.

"Lindsay can cook some good collard greens," Datron said.

"My mama taught Lindsay how to cook like that," Tameka said.

"So you can cook like that too?" Datron asked Tameka.

"Better," Tameka said.

"Oh lord have mercy!" Datron said as they left.

Datron was a big man and he drove a big vehicle. Datron opened the passenger side door of his Mercedes-Benz GLS63 AMG SUV and helped Tameka step inside.

"This is nice and big," Tameka said.

"Well as you can see, I don't fit very well in a small car, so I got this. I like a little get up and go, so I got the high horsepower version," Datron said as the 577 horsepower engine roared to life.

Datron drove to an exclusive steakhouse and got the most secluded table in the restaurant.

"Tameka, thank you for agreeing to come to dinner with me. I would have understood if you had said no given the situation. It's really rough when you realize your marriage is ending when you thought you would be with that person forever," Datron said.

"Yeah, it's rough. I never thought my husband would do what he did to me. You said your marriage ended too. If you don't mind me asking, what happened?" Tameka asked Datron.

"Well, I was playing football in Los Angeles at the time and that's where I met RJ. Anyway, I met Charmane and she was the most beautiful woman I had ever seen. We got together, had a whirlwind romance and within six months we were married. Everything was great for, at least for two years. I was doing my thing playing football and she was crazy about me, or so I thought. One day I was leaving the house to go somewhere and when I finally got all the way to the garage I realized I forgot my keys. I went back upstairs and I guess I left the garage door open so the alarm beep didn't go off. When I go close to the bedroom door I heard her talking on her cell phone. I figured she was talking to her sister or something. Then I heard her say, he's gone right now. I can't wait to see you again. They have an out of town game this weekend. We can meet at your place Saturday night. You know I love how you lick me down there. After I heard that, I went back downstairs and closed the garage entry door so the alarm would beep and went upstairs and got my keys," Datron said.

"What did she say when you came back upstairs?" Tameka asked.

"She played it off like nothing was going on. I left, but instead of going to the store, I called my lawyer and went to his office. I told him what I overheard and he told me to keep cool about it. Well, Charmane handled all the bills and I never paid attention to any of that stuff. I got her cell phone bills and made copies of them and took them to my lawyer. It turned out that there was one number that kept showing up over and over especially when I was on the road. They found out whose number it was, found the address and put a private detective on her. It didn't take long. That weekend while I was in Florida she went to see this guy and they filmed her walking into his house. He answered the door, kissed her and ran his hands all over her behind before she went inside," Datron said.

"Who was he?" Tameka asked.

"His name was Anthony. He was some television producer friend of hers. I guess Charmane thought she could be some kind of reality television star or something. Apparently she had been hooking up with that guy the whole time we were married. I had the divorce papers drawn up and presented them to her. Charmane freaked out and denied everything until I showed her a still shot of her kissing the guy with his hands on her butt. Then she tried to rip my heart out and told me that the only reason she married me was to come up in the world. She said why would a woman that looked the way she did, marry a big dumb ass country guy like me if I wasn't a pro football player and could help her career. I felt like the biggest fool on earth. I thought Charmane really loved me, " Datron said.

"She just came out and said that?" Tameka replied.

"Look, I'm just a simple guy from a little town in Mississippi, back there if you stand in front of God and family and pledge your love in marriage it means something. This using marriage as a stepping stone stuff just blew me away. Anyway we split and I was almost afraid to talk to a woman for a long time. I just didn't trust anybody," Datron said.

Tameka then related to Datron what happened between her and Terrance.

"What a minute. The man knew you had three young children when he met you. Did he think the kids were going to drive themselves around? He wasn't ready to be a real husband or father. When you marry somebody, you marry everything they bring with them including their children if they have any," Datron said.

"Okay Datron, I'm going to confess something. Lindsay told me that you remembered me from her wedding. I was surprised," Tameka said.

"Well there were certain things about you that made an impression on me," Datron said.

"Yeah, she told me about that," Tameka said.

"What do you mean?" Datron asked.

"I guess she heard you say something to RJ about me," Tameka said.

"She heard that. Oh lord, the walls have ears in that house. I didn't mean any disrespect. I was just calling it like I saw it. You got stuck in my head," Datron said.

"I'm not upset about it. A woman likes to be noticed for her assets," Tameka said.

"You see, now you're messing with me. Lindsay told me you were with someone and I left it alone. RJ called me and told me you were here," Datron said.

"What did he say?" Tameka.

"Well he said, 'Hey D. You know Lindsay's friend you saw at my wedding. She's in town. Get your butt over here because they'll be back in a couple of hours. Man you should have saw me getting dressed. I think that was the fastest I've moved since I retired from football," Datron said.

"Really, besides the other thing that caught your attention, why did you want to get to know me?" Tameka asked.

"Well, I saw how happy RJ was after he met Lindsay and found out who she really was. Lindsay told me about how you two were best friends and how you struggled to make it. I figured if he found a woman like Lindsay and you did what you did for her, and then I decided that I needed to know you. Look, I know this is too soon, but I wasn't going to miss an opportunity to know more about you just because of that. I've got time. We can talk on the phone and take it slow," Datron said.

"I don't really know what to say, except thank you. You are a nice guy. We can talk and get to know each other. That would be nice," Tameka said.

Tameka and Datron exchanged phone numbers and enjoyed each other's company along with a great meal. Datron pulled up to the Jefferson's home and walked Tameka to the front door.

"Tameka, I had a great time. I know you'll be going back home soon," Datron said.

"I enjoyed being with you tonight. It was fun. Thanks for asking me out. I guess I better get inside," Tameka said.

"Okay. I'll talk to you later," Datron said as he was about to leave.

Tameka turned around and walked up to Datron and gave him a kiss on the cheek and a hug. Datron hugged her back.

"Everything's going to work out," Datron said before Tameka went inside.

Before she knew it Tameka and her three children were driving back to Texas and reality.

5

Tameka went back home and got back into her routine as a newly single woman. Although Tameka didn't want anything to do with Terrance again, she missed being married and was reminded of that void every time she came home. Tameka's adult conversations with Terrance were replaced by asking her children about their school activities. Tameka talked with Lindsay often by telephone, but became self-conscious of monopolizing too much of her dear friend's time. Tameka managed to stay busy during the day, but it was at night when she went to bed that the reality that one side of her king size bed was now empty hit her the hardest.

Although her family went from a group of five to four with her as the leader, Tameka was determined to take her family in the right direction. Going to church with her children was one routine Tameka was determined to maintain. Although church was a place for spiritual renewal, it could also be a place for harsh judgment from others. Tameka still met and sat with her mother at church along with her children. One Sunday Tameka met her mother at the front steps of the modestly sized church.

"Mama, go ahead and take them in with you while I use the bathroom. I'll be inside in a minute. Ya'll sit down and be still and mind you grandma," Tameka admonished.

"They know they better behave inside the lord's house. Don't you?" Sonya said as she shot a look at her grandchildren.

"Yes ma'am," they all said in chorus.

Tameka went into the women's bathroom that was on one side of the foyer that led to the doors of the sanctuary. Tameka was sitting on the toilet when she heard two women talking just outside.

"Who was that woman that just walked in here ahead of us with those three children? They were so cute," one woman said.

A smile crossed Tameka's face at the complement directed at her children, but her smile would be short lived.

"Girl, that's Sonya Davis and her three grandchildren," another woman said.

"That was Deacon Davis' wife? I didn't recognize her in that dress. It must be new," the first woman said.

"I hadn't seen it before," the second woman said.

"Those are her daughter Tameka's kids. Child, I heard each one of them is by a different man," the first woman said.

"Are you serious?" the second woman said.

"As a heart attack. She left home with none, came back with three and no husband. I guess she couldn't keep her legs closed," the first woman said.

"She did get married, didn't she?" one of the women asked.

"She was, until he left. I don't know what happened, but what man wants a ready-made family? That's a lot to take on, taking care of other men's children," the first woman said.

Tameka was experiencing an emotional cocktail of sadness, embarrassment and anger. Tameka thought, how dare they pass judgment on her family while standing right outside the doors of a church sanctuary. Tameka decided that she had enough. Tameka opened the bathroom door, stepped outside and was looking both women in the eyes. Tameka was surprised at the identity of her detractors, Davita Brooks and Vicki Jones. Vicki was an old friend of Tameka's mother and Davita was, of all people, Keisha's mother.

"Hi, Tameka, I was just telling Davita how cute your children looked when they went inside the church with Sonya," Vicki said.

"Well thank you. You know two of them look like me and the other one looks like his father," Tameka said.

The women seemed taken aback by Tameka response. Tameka then turned to Vicki.

"Miss Brooks, did Keisha come to church with you today?" Tameka asked.

"No. Keisha didn't come. She said she had something else she needed to do," Vicki said.

"I understand, Keisha is always busy doing somebody, I mean something. I've got to get inside and help mama with all those kids. Enjoy the service ladies," Tameka said as she walked inside.

Vicki and Davita stood there and looked at each other in embarrassment.

"Oh Jesus! I didn't know she was in that bathroom. I think she heard us," Vicki remarked in a whisper before they went inside.

6

Tameka was not about to allow the judgments of town gossips like Davita and Vicki cause her to hang her head in shame, because they like most others failed to see their own faults. Davita got pregnant with Keisha as a teenager after she had an affair with a married man. Vicki Jones was also far from a saint considering she had regular visits from a married man every Wednesday night while his wife attended mid-week church services. Vicki always told everyone they were just friends, but that contention went out of the window after they were caught in the act behind a night club in Kilgore, Texas after having one too many drinks one night.

Vicki considered herself a social butterfly of sorts in the local black community. Vicki spent part of her young adult years as a high school teacher in California and some locals thought that caused her to be more fashionable and worldly than those who never left the area. After her parents died in a tragic car accident Vicki came back home and the black men around town found her fascinating. Vicki was a stunning young woman and even at the age of fifty she was still well put together with a slender figure and light skin tone. Vicki made sure she went out in public in figure flattering clothes, flawless makeup and heels. No one knew how she met her special friend, but he was a manufacturing plant manager and everyone knew he was married. Tameka was not a big fan of Vicki because she thought she flaunted herself a little too flirtatiously in front of her father. Vicki seemed to wear her shortest skirts, tightest pants and highest heels when she visited her friend Sonya. Vicki would often stand with her butt in Tameka's father's face or cross her legs excessively when she was around him. Tameka even told her mother to watch out for Vicki, but Sonya dismissed her concerns. For his part, Gregory Davis would usually leave the room whenever Vicki came around. Tameka didn't know that her father told his wife that he knew exactly what Vicki was up too and they both thought it was comical.

Vicki was usually careful with her most private activities, but that night at the club she let her hair and guard down. Someone walked by her friend's luxury sports utility vehicle that was parked behind the club an unusually long distance away from other vehicles. As the man approached the vehicle on his way to smoke a cigarette, a noise startled him. He walked over to the vehicle and looked inside. To his surprise he was looking Vicki directly in her face. Vicki's eyes were closed, but she was on her hands and knees on the middle bench seat of the vehicle. Her friend was positioned on his knees behind her with his hands on her shoulders and his eyes looking upward at the headliner of his SUV. Vicki's body moved forward with each thrust he made into her from behind. Vicki's dress was bunched around her waist exposing her lower body and breasts that were swinging with each movement. The man knew exactly who she was because he lived around the corner from her in the same neighborhood. Before the night was over it was all over town thatMiss

Thing was caught getting fucked on the back seat of a car parked behind a seedy nightclub by a married man.

The strange thing is that Vicki never knew she was caught in the act, but everyone else did, Vicki's indiscretion became one of those unspoken pieces of public knowledge that made her the butt of jokes while she thought she was held in the highest of esteem.

Tameka knew that both Vicki and Davita were first class hypocrites throwing stones at easy targets, but with knowledge of Vicki's recent slip-up it made it all the worse. Tameka also knew others would pass judgment and place blame on her for her marriage failing. In that small town Tameka couldn't hide in the crowd or relocate to an area where she wasn't known. Tameka decided to live in her truth because she realized she made mistakes in the past, but so did others. Although she made missteps, Tameka didn't view the children who came from her poor judgment as mistakes, but as her greatest joy. Tameka's children were respectful, well behaved and intelligent. Tameka's biggest regret was watching them cope with confusion after her marriage to Terrance fell apart. The man her kids called daddy was gone and she saw the pain in their eyes. Children are resilient and Tameka's were no different as they adjusted to her as the single head of household once again.

Although her children bounced back quickly, Tameka couldn't say the same for herself. Although Terrance had been gone for a while, Tameka still felt like she was missing half of her being and was experiencing a special kind of loneliness that work, her children and a busy schedule were unable to fill.

Tameka lay in bed one night after her children were sound asleep. The sounds of crickets, night birds and a dog's distant bark were her background sound track. Soft moonlight came through the semicircular window positioned above the main bedroom windows. Times such as those were when Tameka missed the intimate touch of a man the most. Still vibrant and in her twenties, Tameka sometimes felt the rest of the world was passing her by while she simply marked time. That night was different as Tameka felt she was in a state of social limbo. What she had with Datron was new and remote and what she shared with a man she once loved was now a memory.

Tameka's hands migrated down her body and passed over her still taught abdomen. With her fingers slipping under the elastic waistband of her panties, Tameka felt her own moistness. With her mind guiding her hands, Tameka played a sensual melody on her sexual instrument. Tameka knew what she liked, but she would rather have someone else providing it, but this time her self-pleasuring would have to suffice. After discarding her underwear completely, Tameka really focused on the task at hand with her legs spread and drawn back. Tameka's fingers were concentrating on her pleasure center. With her breathing quickening, Tameka suddenly clasped her legs together around her hand while rolling on her side quivering in silence. After her heart rate returned to normal,

Tameka felt a tear roll down her face and decided something had to change in her life.

7

Datron and Tameka talked often on the phone and random surprise gifts would arrive for her at the office. Datron was not the only man interested in Tameka as one of her coworkers was making his intentions known. Braeland Kelly was a twenty-three year old field inspector in the Department of Social Services office where Tameka was a supervisor. Braeland was a handsome young man, standing over six feet tall with a muscular build, but he was several years younger than Tameka, so she never looked at him as a potential romantic partner. Other women around the office took notice of Braeland and he basked in their attention, but Braeland liked a challenge and Tameka was on his mind.

"How are you doing Miss Davis?" Braeland said as he walked into the break room.

"Hey, Braeland, I'm doing okay. How about you?" Tameka said.

"I'm fine. Do you mind if I sit with you for lunch?" Braeland asked.

"Go ahead and take a seat," Tameka said.

"I wanted to ask you something?" Braeland said.

"What's that," Tameka said.

"Suppose I asked you out, like on a date or something, what would you say," Braeland asked.

Tameka stopped her spoon in mid motion as she was about to take a bite.

"Braeland, are you serious. You've asked me out before, but I thought you were just playing around?" Tameka said.

"Naw, I'm serious," Braeland said.

"Why would you want to take me out on a date?" Tameka said.

Braeland looked around.

"Well, you're the best looking woman in here. You're nice. You care about the people that come in here for help. You don't just show up to pick up a paycheck. I like that. Maybe we could go to the movies or something," Braeland said.

"I'm a little old for you aren't I?" Tameka said.

"What, you must be about twenty five, that's just a couple of years apart," Braeland said.

"I'm twenty-eight, that's about five years older than you," Tameka said.

"Twenty eight! You're the best looking twenty-eight year old woman I've seen in a long time," Braeland said.

"Well thank you. You know I've got three kids don't you," Tameka said.

"Yeah, I know that. I saw them at the office Christmas party. They're nice kids," Braeland said.

"I don't want to go to the movies with you Braeland," Tameka said.

"Okay, I understand. I just thought I'd ask, again" Braeland said with a sound of disappointment in his voice.

"I like to dance. I want to go to a club and dance a little. How about Saturday night? My mother will keep my kids," Tameka said.

44

"For real! I can handle that. Give me your address and I'll pick you up," Braeland said with a smile on his face.

Tameka gave Braeland her address and phone number so he could call her if something came up at the last minute. Braeland walked out of the room with an energized stride. Tameka almost laughed to herself at his excitement. Six months after her divorce, Tameka was going out on her second date. Rose Brown, Tameka's coworker and friend, walked in and sat down with Tameka to eat her lunch.

"Hey Tameka, what's going on with you? Why do you have that big smile on your face?" Rose asked.

"I have a date this weekend," Tameka said.

"Really, with who?! Is that guy that sends you flowers all the time?" Rose asked.

"No, it's not him," Tameka answered.

"Don't make me drag it out of you. Who's the mystery man?" Rose inquired.

"I guess I'm going out on a date with Braeland this weekend," Tameka said.

"What? Excuse me. Did you say you were going out on a date with Braeland? The Braeland that works here?" Rose said.

"He asked me out. I thought about it and said yes," Tameka said.

"I can't believe you're going out with him. I mean he fine and all, but he's a little young for you, isn't he?" Rose said.

"Well Rose, do you see men knocking my door down asking me out. I do want to have some fun every once in a while," Tameka said.

"What about that guy that sends you all those gifts and flowers?" Rose asked.

"He's not here is he? Talking on the telephone and getting flowers only goes so far. If he wants something to happen it's going to take more than that. A man should know what he has to do. I shouldn't have to tell him," Tameka declared.

"Well, I hope you know what you're doing. I hear Braeland's a player who likes to spread his stuff around and has quite a reputation with women," Rose said.

"I've heard all about that. I'm not really interested in Braeland. I feel like I just need to get out of this cycle I'm in. All I do is work, take care of my kids and keep my house in order the best I can. I go to sleep exhausted. I'm tired and need a break. This will be something different to do for a change. I like to dance and have fun too. This isn't like a real date anyway. Braeland is too young for me, but it will be interesting to see what these younger people do when they go out," Tameka said.

"Okay. You can tell me what they do, because I can't even understand anything those rappers are saying on some of the songs my kids listen to at home," Rose remarked.

Tameka found herself putting in a surprising amount of effort in preparation for her outing with Braeland. Although she didn't consider going out with Braeland a serious date in the sense of viewing him as a potential boyfriend or husband for that

46

matter, Tameka still wanted to look her best. It had been a while since she got dressed up for anything other than work and church. With her children safe with their grandparents, Tameka put the finishing touches on her hair and makeup. Tameka stood in front of the full length mirror mounted on the bathroom door and reviewed the finished product. Tameka recalled those days when she used to hit the clubs in Dallas several years earlier. With her hair pulled back and hanging to shoulder level, figure hugging skirt and top, Tameka declared she was ready for public viewing. With her six inch heel on, Tameka figured she would be looking six-foot two inch tall Braeland in his eyes. Tameka decided what she saw confirmed she still had what it took to turn any man's head.

Tameka's phone received an incoming call from Braeland telling her he was almost there. Braeland pulled up in Tameka's driveway around nine o'clock and she almost passed out when she saw his car.

"What the hell is that all about?" Tameka said under her breath.

Braeland was driving his baby, a Chrysler 300 Hemi with candy apple red paint that looked like you could dive into it. Braeland's car had a window tint that had to be too dark to be legal and it was sitting on twenty-six inch chrome rims with low profile tires. Tameka walked outside. Braeland came around and opened Tameka's door which went upward instead of opening the way it did from the factory.

"Damn, you're on point! Tameka you look like a different person. I figured I should call you Tameka instead of Miss Davis since we're going out together," Braeland said.

"Braeland, this car is really something. This isn't what you drive to work," Tameka said.

"Oh no. I only drive this when I'm off and on weekends. I don't want to get it scratched at work. That's why I drive that little car every day. This is my baby here. I save it for special occasions and honeys like you," Braeland said.

"Okay, so you consider me to be a honey? I'll take that as a complement. Where are we going?" Tameka said.

"We're going to the Ebony Essence Club in Longview. They've got a good DJ over there. He keeps it lit," Braeland said as he stole a glance at Tameka's long legs.

Tameka assumed she was dressed appropriately for the occasion with her short tight black skirt, six inch heels and a white form fitting top. Braeland was wearing a pair of loose fitting jeans, a white shirt and a pair of sneakers. When they arrived at the club, Tameka could tell that she was at the top of the age range of the clientele in the place. Once inside they found a table about twenty feet from the dance floor and below the DJ booth.

"Do you want something to drink?" Braeland asked as a waitress came by.

Tameka ordered a glass of wine and Braeland ordered a beer.

"This place is pretty nice," Tameka said.

Hip hop seemed to be the music style this DJ preferred and he dimmed the lights about the time their drinks arrived. Three young women took to the dance floor with their backs to most of the seating area and a strip club anthem type rap song blasted from the speakers. The women started to bounce their butts in rhythm to the beat and it was obvious that they had rehearsed their dance together.

"What the hell are they doing taking over the dance floor?" Tameka asked.

"That's Yolanda, Alicia and Kalinda. They put together a twerk team. This is the twerk contest night. Different groups of individuals will go up and twerk and then the audience votes by applause. The winners get a prize of about two hundred dollars," Braeland said.

Tameka was enjoying herself more than she expected. Just being in a different environment was refreshing. Braeland surprised her with a conversation level deeper that what she expected. Being in a playground designed for adults to shed some of their stress and inhibitions did wonders for Tameka's mood.

As the night went on Tameka kept downing more glasses of wine and was starting to get a good buzz. After the twerk contest was finished, Braeland asked Tameka to dance and she managed to keep up with the group. It didn't seem that people were actually dancing as Tameka observed, but the women seemed to be rubbing their butts against the groins of their male partners. After a nonstop feed of hip hop the music changed to a slow song that

Tameka recognized. Braeland turned Tameka around and started to slow dance.

"Braeland, you know how to slow dance?" Tameka asked.

"Yeah, I know how to slow drag," Braeland said as he ground his pelvis into Tameka.

By this time Tameka was feeling no pain due to her alcohol consumption and had her arms draped around Braeland's neck as she ground her pelvis into his body. Heat from all the other bodies on the dance floor helped enhance the effects of Tameka's wine intake as it affected her body and mind. Braeland slid his hands down Tameka's back and each one cupped one of her ass cheeks. No effort came from Tameka to remove Braeland's hands and he decided to squeeze the bounty in his grasp. Tameka responded by resting her head on his shoulder. Tameka also felt something else pressing into her body from the front that told her that Braeland was interested in more than just dancing.

"Let's get out of here," Braeland said in Tameka's ear.

"Okay," Tameka replied.

Braeland lived about ten miles from the club and he stopped by his place and invited Tameka inside. As they closed the door, Braeland turned on some music and pulled Tameka close and kissed her. Tameka looked at Braeland with a look that seemed to be full of questions about the next action she took.

"Braeland, what are you doing?" Tameka said with a glazed look in her eyes.

50

Braeland didn't say a word and kissed Tameka again. Tameka responded by kissing him back forcefully. Braeland ran his tongue down Tameka's neck as he palmed her firm buttocks. "Oh Jesus, Braeland, I don't know if we should be doing this. You know we work together," Tameka said weakly.

Braeland didn't answer initially, but instead, he placed one hand under her top and squeezed Tameka's breasts while his other hand went under her skirt rubbing her panty covered crotch. "Come on baby, you know you want this," Braeland said.

No objection came from Tameka's lips as she thrust her hips back and forth to match Braeland's hand motions. Braeland unbuttoned Tameka's blouse and pulled her bra down as he shifted his oral attention to her breasts. Tameka was fighting a losing battle against six months of pent up sexual tension, wine and a man pushing every button she had. Braeland was young, but he knew his way around a woman's body. Braeland removed Tameka's blouse, unsnapped her bra and she was soon naked from the waist up. Moving behind Tameka as she braced for balance in her half inebriated state with her hands holding onto the back of the sofa, Braeland reached under Tameka's short skirt and pulled her panties down and they fell to the floor as Tameka stepped out of them with her heels still on. Braeland knew Tameka was at a point of no return. Braeland reached around and fondled Tameka's breasts with one hand as she instinctively ground her ass into Braeland's groin. Braeland's

51

other hand found its way into the moist valley between Tameka's thighs. Braeland dropped to his knees behind Tameka and soon he tasted the sweet nectar of this mature woman.

"Oh shit!" Tameka exclaimed as she pushed her body back into Braeland's face.

Tameka gripped the leather sofa for support with her legs quivering and felt like electric shocks were running through her body. Braeland then stood up behind Tameka and fondled her breasts once more. Tameka reached around and unfastened Braeland's pants and felt them fall to the floor.

"Braeland, quit playing. If you're going to fuck me, come on," Tameka said as she rubbed against his stiff member still encased in his underwear.

Braeland was a little surprised by her statement, but he pulled his underwear down and slowly probed for Tameka's wetness as she spread her legs apart and leaned forward on the back of the sofa. Braeland grabbed two handfuls of Tameka's ass cheeks for leverage and slowly moved forward until his pelvis made contact with her buttocks.

"Oh fuck! That's what I'm talking about," Tameka said as she pressed her body back into Braeland's.

Using Tameka's waist as a point of control Braeland began to thrust into Tameka as she met him at each point of impact. Soon there was a rhythm of colliding flesh as Tameka satisfied months of sexual deprivation all at one time. It wasn't too long before Tameka reached her boiling point.

"Ohh! Ohh! I'm coming! Ohhh shit!" Tameka said as Braeland smacked her ass with his hand and joined her.

Tameka collapsed across the back of the sofa with Braeland draped across her back. Braeland slowly stood and stumbled backwards. Tameka crawled over the back of the sofa and stretched out on the seat cushions as Braeland came back with a towel and bottles of water. They were both drenched with sweat. Braeland sat on the edge of the sofa while Tameka was lying there naked and rubbed his back.

"Braeland, that was so good. You know this is what it is. We're not going to be together as a couple or anything," Tameka said.

"Yeah, I know. You're not like those young girls I go out with. You're a grown woman. I didn't think that you would even go out with me, let along we end up doing this together," Braeland said.

"That's right Braeland, I'm a grown ass woman and I only do something if I want to. I wanted to do this, yeah the wine helped me along, but mama got to have some fun too, you know, but I didn't just use you for sex," Tameka said smiling.

"Hold up, use me? That's usually what women usually ask me. If that's the case, you can do like that old song says and use me up," Braeland said laughing.

"Oh really, what do you know about that song?" Tameka said as she sat up and pulled Braeland down on the sofa.

"What are you doing?" Braeland said.

53

"Just like you said, I'm going to use you up tonight," Tameka said as she moved downward on Braeland's body.

Braeland felt Tameka's hot, moist breath on the most sensitive spot on his body.

"Shit Tameka, you do know how to do that shit, don't you. Damn, your top game is strong," Braeland stated as he looked up at the ceiling.

"Braeland, I know things those young girls you mess with haven't found out yet. I just don't broadcast it. Let me get this thing just right so you can just lay there while I ride it where I want to go," Tameka said as she readied Braeland for one last round of torrid sex.

"Goddamn! Ride that dick bitch!" Braeland said as Tameka rocked on top of his body with her head thrown back.

Tameka was in another world and normally someone calling her a bitch would get a swift negative reaction, but nothing Braeland said even registered. Braeland's words were just background noise because at that point he was just an instrument being used for her physical pleasure. That night Tameka did use Braeland up until he could not rise to the occasion any longer. Braeland tapped out and finally took Tameka home with his ego both inflated and bruised at the same time.

The next day Tameka woke up at home and had a pounding headache.

"Shit, my head," Tameka said as she sat up in bed then she remembered everything that happened the night before, except how she got from Braeland's car to her bed.

Tameka went to her kitchen and drank a glass of orange juice, before cooking bacon and eggs for breakfast. Tameka's children were still over at her parent's home and were going to church with their grandparents who would drop them by her house on the way back from services. After an hour or so Tameka started to feel better and picked up her cell phone.

"Hey Lindsay, how are you?" Tameka said.

"Tameka, you sound like shit, what's going on?" Lindsay asked.

"I think I screwed up big time. I went out with this young guy at work last night. I drank a little too much and ending up fucking him," Tameka said.

"What, you had sex with somebody you work with? You said he was young, how young?" Lindsay asked.

"About twenty three," Tameka said.

"That's pretty damn young. How was it?" Lindsay asked.

"How was it? Shit, it was great. He was knocking my back out, but that's not the point. I'm a manager at that place and I see this guy every day at work. He used to call me Miss Davis and now it will be like, that's the bitch I fucked. That was so stupid. I got drunk, was horny and bam, it happened," Tameka said.

"Look, you'll survive this. It might be a little awkward around work for a while, but that will pass. What about you and Datron?" Lindsay asked.

"Datron is not around. I talk to him on the phone and he sends me gifts, but he may as well be a million miles away. I love talking to him, but without seeing him and getting to know him, I can't build a real relationship with him. When RJ got serious about you, he invited you up to see him at his house," Tameka said.

"Yeah, but that was different, because we had a son together already and he wanted to get to know Riley. Look Datron is a really nice guy, maybe too nice, what if you made the first move and invited him to come down there and visit you. He can stay at a hotel, but spend time with you so two could really get to know each other. He said he would give you time, maybe you need to let him know that the time is now. Women don't have to wait on a man to make every move anymore. Look at me, if I didn't decide it was time that RJ knew he had a son, I wouldn't be with him today," Lindsay said.

"I'll think about what you said. It makes a lot of sense. Thanks Lindsay, love you," Tameka said.

"Love you too Tameka, everything will be okay," Lindsay said as she ended the call.

"RJ!" Lindsay called out.

RJ came around the corner.

"What is it?" RJ asked.

"RJ, you need to talk to your boy Datron. What the hell is wrong with him? He says he's really interested in getting to know Tameka, but he's letting her swing in the wind down there in east Texas. She hadn't seen him not one time in the six months since she was up here. He needs to get his big ass down there and see her. She's not going to

56

wait on his ass forever. Light a fire under his ass and tell him if he's interested in my friend, then either shit or get off the pot. You know what I'm saying?" Lindsay said.

"All right I'll holler at him about it. You know he's kind of reserved, he was an offensive lineman you know," RJ said.

"What! What kind of crazy shit is that? Just talk to his ass, that's all," Lindsay said as she went upstairs.

8

Tameka went to work on Monday full of dread that she would run into Braeland before he went into the field, but she made it to her office without an uncomfortable encounter. Around ten in the morning, Tameka realized that she had left a file in her car that she needed to review and she went downstairs to get it. As Tameka approached the edge of the building to go around the corner to the parking lot she heard two men talking and recognized their voices. One man was Melvin Parker, a senior field inspector and the other voice was Braeland's. Tameka stopped in her tracks.

"Braeland, are you getting ready to do some visits?" Melvin said.

"Yeah, I got a full slate today," Braeland said.

"How was your weekend? Did you knock down some fresh pussy," Melvin asked.

"Yeah, but this was a good one. You know Tameka Davis who works upstairs don't you?" Datron said.

"What, the case intake manager? Yeah I know her. What about it?" Melvin asked.

"I took her out Saturday night," Braeland said.

"What! You're fucking with me right? Isn't she married with kids?" Melvin asked.

"No, she got divorced about six months ago. I heard her talking to Miss Rose about it. I asked her out last week and she said yes," Braeland said.

"So you took her out, what happened?" Melvin asked.

"What do you think, I hit that pussy good, backshots, the whole thing," Datron said.

Tameka was quaking with anger and embarrassment that Braeland would spread her intimate business like that.

"You've got to be lying. You're kidding me, right?" Melvin quizzed with and unbelieving look on his face.

"Naw dog. I'm for real on this," Braeland assured.

"What the hell is a backshot?" Melvin asked

"That's when you fuck a woman from behind. I love that because you can spank that ass a couple of times and sometimes you just let them do all the work while you stand there and chill. She gave me good top too. That bitch has a killer head game. That's why I love baby mamas man. They don't get regular dick when they want it because of their kids being around most of the time, but if you take them out, they're ready to fuck, but need a little something to get them ready. A few drinks, weed or whatever they're into and it's on man. Shit, I've got four or five baby mamas I hit on a regular basis, but this was a one-time thing. I've wanted that ass for a long time. She's got that good experienced pussy too," Braeland said.

"I'm just surprised that she would go out with you and do all that, but I guess you can't read a book by its cover," Melvin said.

"What, you think she's too good for me or something. Let me tell you something man, a lot of these women walking around with their nose stuck up in the air because of their job title, money or family they come from are straight up freaks if you get them alone somewhere where no one else is around to see them. I know, and Tameka was no different. A little dancing, a lot of wine and that shit was lit," Braeland informed.

"Braeland, let me give you a little advice. Don't tell this to anyone else. What you do out there is one thing, but you work here. Have you ever heard the term, don't shit where you eat. That means don't make things uncomfortable in places that you go to regularly like your job or home. Miss Davis has worked here for a while and in her position, you wouldn't want to piss her off, so beat your chest at home and leave it there," Melvin said.

Tameka hurried back upstairs, went into her office and locked the door. Grabbing a handful of tissues from her box, Tameka burst out crying as she barely held herself together long enough to get out of the view of everyone else. Tameka thought that Braeland was an immature asshole and she was pissed at herself for getting involved with him. The thing that cut Tameka the deepest were his words about single mothers because they reminded her of what her ex-husband Terrance said when she threw him out. Terrance's words rang loudly in Tameka's mind, 'With three kids, ain't no other man going to be looking at you for nothing but a quick fuck as a side hoe' she recalled. Braeland's actions were even worse than what Terrance said, because even side chicks had some kind of commitment from a man. Braeland simply used single mothers as easy sexual targets. The more Tameka thought about what she heard, the angrier she became and then a knock came at her office door. Tameka made sure her she dried the tears from her face before answering.

"Come in," Tameka answered.

Rose came in through the door.

"Tameka, what's going on? I didn't see you in the break room for lunch and you're sitting here in your office with the door closed. You know I'm dying to know how your date went with Braeland," Rose said.

Tameka took a deep breath while Rose sat down across from her.

"Oh Rose. The club was great. We talked, we danced and we drank. I had a lot of fun, but things changed after we left the club," Tameka said.

"Things changed. What do you mean?" Rose asked.

"Well you know I didn't really take that date with Braeland seriously, but things changed after we went to his apartment," Tameka said.

"What? You went to Braeland's apartment?" Rose said surprised.

"I didn't plan to, but the wine and everything else got to me. Well you know how things can change when someone is not thinking straight. One thing kind of led to another," Tameka said.

Rose looked at Tameka in amazement with her mouth hanging open.

"Tameka don't tell me that…" Rose said before Tameka cut her off.

"That I had sex with him. Well I did. I was high from drinking and he was all over me. I was weak and needy. Braeland was a man I could touch right then, so he touched me in the way a woman needs to be touched. I'm a grown woman. Braeland didn't force himself on me. At that time, I wanted it. I needed it, but he was the wrong one," Tameka said.

"I'm just shocked. I never thought you would end up having sex with him, but what do you mean he was the wrong one?" Rose inquired.

"He has the mind of a teenage boy and has to brag to someone about all the women he has sex with. This was a one-time thing anyway, but now I know it was a big mistake," Tameka admitted.

"Did he tell someone about being with you?" Rose asked.

"He couldn't wait. I overhead him telling Mr. Parker about it in the parking lot," Tameka said.

"Melvin Parker? What did he tell him?" Rose asked.

"He told him everything and talked about me like I was a piece of meat. He said that as a single mother, or baby mama as he called me, I was in his target group for easy sex and was just one of a string of single mothers he's having or has had sex with. Unwed mothers make up a lot of the client base this agency serves. I interview them every day; he's just a predator preying on their vulnerabilities. Braeland told him everything in the dirtiest way he could. It was so embarrassing, but Mr. Parker tried to talk some sense into him. I just hoped he listened," Tameka said.

"Tameka, I don't pass judgment on people, it's above my pay grade. What's done is done, but you can't come in to work every day hoping Braeland got the message. You need to tell him face to face how things are going to go and shut his little ass down. This is your job here. You're in management and make good money that takes care of your kids. It's not like you can get another job making this much money around here if you lost this one. If he runs his mouth to the wrong person you could both be out of here. Handle it. I've got to get back to work, but you need to take care of this as soon as possible," Rose said as she left Tameka's office.

Tameka knew Rose was right and she had to confront Braeland for the sake of her job and future. The only question Tameka had was how and where she would do it. There were too many eyes to see and ears to hear at her job. Tameka decided to strike while the iron was hot and determined the best place would be where the issue arose the first time, Braeland's apartment. Tameka had Braeland's phone number in her phone from when he called her letting her know he was on his way to pick her up before they went out the prior Saturday night. Tameka sent a text message to Braeland asking to meet him at his place after work. Braeland quickly replied yes. Braeland's last visit was not far from his apartment so he would be there before Tameka arrived.

Tameka made it through to the end of the day, but she vowed to never put herself in a position like she did with Braeland again because her reputation was at stake and she had to think of how something like that could affect her children. With that on her mind, Tameka made the drive to the place where she did something she wanted to do at the time, but now the risk of it getting out was too great. Tameka walked up the stairs and knocked on Braeland's apartment door.

"Tameka, come on in," Braeland said when he opened the door.

"I guess you're wondering why I wanted to come over," Tameka said.

"I know why you came over. You want some more of this," Braeland said as he grabbed his manhood through his pants.

"No, that's not why I wanted to come over and it's back to Miss Davis to you," Tameka said.

"Miss Davis?! I wasn't calling you Miss Davis when you were bent over this sofa while I was dicking you down last Saturday night," Braeland reminded.

"Okay Braeland, we both know we had sex that night and now Mr. Parker knows because you couldn't keep your mouth shut," Tameka said.

"What?! Did he tell you what I said?!" Braeland asked.

"He didn't have to. I was going out to my car and heard everything you said. You were out there acting like some high school kid bragging about screwing the head cheerleader. Braeland,we both work there! I don't want to lose my job and I know you don't want to lose yours," Tameka said.

"How am I going to lose my job by telling the truth? You gave up the pussy and that's what happened. That didn't have anything to do with work. I know you're a manager at work, but that night you were riding my dick and begging for more!" Braeland said.

"Okay Braeland, I only thought you were an asshole, but you just confirmed it. I tried to be nice about this, but you don't understand nice. Our agency has a code of conduct that everyone that works there signed. One of the provisions of that code of conduct is avoiding inappropriate relationships with the clients we serve. It's seems that some the baby mamas you're having sex with, as you told Mr. Parker, are our clients that you met while doing on the job visits. I think that qualifies as inappropriate relationships," Tamkea said.

"How do you know that?" Braeland asked with a shaky tone in his voice.

"You log every visit in our system. People know everything about each other around there. You have some visits that take over an hour and a half when most take thirty minutes. Those visits are taking place when the clients' children are at school, so what are you checking on for that long, the house, living conditions or the client's bedroom skills. I can get your ass fired in a second. Do we have an understanding that not one word of what happened between us in this apartment will come out of your mouth again, or do I call those client's up and do an investigation," Tameka asked.

Braeland swallowed hard.

"Yeah," Braeland replied.

"Yeah what?" Tameka asked.

"I won't say anything else about what happened between us," Braeland said.

"Okay, just as long as we understand each other. By the way, you said I was begging for it. If I remember correctly it got to a point where you just couldn't deliver anymore. Bye Braeland. See you at work tomorrow," Tamkea said.

"Bye Miss Davis," Braeland said.

Braeland watched Tameka walk down the stairs and closed his door.

"Bitch!" Braeland said to himself as he flopped down on his sofa.

On the way home Tameka received a call from Datron and a pleasant surprise. Datron wanted to come down to east Texas and visit Tameka for a week, but he wanted to give her a month's lead time so she could plan for taking some time off from work. Datron said he would be there on a Wednesday so she would only have to take three days off if they counted the weekend.

Tameka's day went from being a horrible experience to having something to look forward to in a matter of minutes.

9

In smaller towns it seemed to be impossible to ever escape all of the ghosts from one's past and it was no different for Tameka as she would occasionally see Keisha or Terrance around town. Seeing Terrance was particularly troubling, because his life went into a downward spiral after their divorce. The county targeted Terrance for having his lunchtime fling while he was driving the county vehicle and eventually found a legitimate reason to oust him from his position. Terrance was having difficulty finding employment with a similar income level and since he was unable to meet his financial obligations he moved back in with his mother after losing his apartment lease. Although Terrance betrayed her trust in the worst way, Tameka didn't enjoy seeing him suffer.

Tameka hadn't run into Keisha since that one incident downtown, but she knew at some point or another she would encounter her again and it happened inside a local grocery store. Tameka was shopping before she went to her mother's house to pick up her children and she saw Keisha walk by the front of a grocery aisle pushing a shopping cart.

"Tameka, girl is that you?" a woman's voice said from behind.

"Anita! Girl, I haven't seen you in forever. Where have you been?" Tameka said.

"Well, I got a job out at the prison and since I was new I got the night shift, so I've been living like a vampire, up all night and sleeping all day. I finally moved to a day shift, but my body clock is still all messed up," Anita said.

"Well, at least we have good jobs. How's Montel? You guys have been together since high school," Tameka asked.

"Huh. He found something else to do while I was working nights. I caught his ass red handed with that hoe we went to school with, Keisha. I took lunch early one night and went home. That bitch's car was pulled up behind my house trying to hide it from being seen from the street. Okay, so I got out and walked around by the bedroom. I heard Montel and Keisha inside," Anita said in a hushed tone.

"I just saw that hoe walk by a few minutes ago," Tameka informed.

"Who, Keisha? She's in here?" Anita asked.

"Yes, she walked by the front of the ailse, so what were they saying?" Tameka asked in a low voice.

"They weren't saying shit, they were fucking," Anita whispered.

"That bitch is going to get hers. That's why I'm divorced now. My ex-husband was messing with her too," Tameka whispered as she looked around.

"I don't get it. The bitch looks like ten miles of bad road. Why are all these men running behind her stank ass? What, does she have gold in her pussy or something?" Anita said.

"She's just a low life hoe that brings out the dog in the men she's with. If a man's dick has an itch, Keisha's there ready to scratch it. She's got a damn open sign flashing on her pussy and waits to see who's ready to come in," Tameka said.

"Girl you're so crazy," Anita said.

"Did you say something to Montel about it?" Tameka asked.

"No, they don't know that I know what's going on, but they will soon. Hey, look at me running my mouth. I've got to get out of here. It was good to see you again. We need to visit sometime soon," Anita said.

"Okay, bye Anita," Tameka said as they hugged.

Tameka finished shopping and pushed her buggy up to the checkout counter that only had one lane open.

"Really," Tameka remarked to a lady in front of her in line and the woman nodded in agreement.

"Hi, Tameka," a voice behind her said.

Tameka turned around and Keisha was standing there with a shopping cart and a smile on her face. Tameka looked around and quickly flashed an upraised middle finger salute to Keisha and silently mouthed the word 'bitch' when she saw Anita walk up behind Keisha. Anita was not pushing a buggy. Tameka saw Anita reach into her purse and recognized the barrel of a gun as she pulled it out. Keisha saw the look of alarm on Tameka's face and she turned around. Keisha found herself looking into the barrel of a 9 millimeter semiautomatic pistol. Keisha was frozen with fear and unable to speak.

"Your days of fucking other women's husbands are over, bitch!" Anita said as she pulled the trigger.

Tameka screamed as the blast from the gun echoed throughout the store. Keisha fell back onto her shopping cart and pushed it into Tameka. The checkout clerk and the woman in front of Tameka screamed and dropped to the floor. Tameka felt something wet on her face. Tameka looked down and her blouse was splattered with blood. Tameka was in shock and Keisha fell to the floor.

"Bang, bang, bang," came as Anita unloaded three more rounds into Keisha's body. Tameka looked up at Anita with her eyes wide and mouth hanging open.

"I got that bitch! Tameka, I got that bitch! I followed your hoe ass in here and caught you slipping bitch!" Anita said as she looked down at Keisha.

"No. Anita, no!" Tameka said through tears.

"Keisha wasn't nothing but a stank hoe anyway. She fucked your husband and mine. Who knows how many marriages this hoe broke up. This was like doing the public a service. Stupid bitch!" Anita said as she spat on Keisha's body that was lying in an expanding pool of blood.

Suddenly the wail of police sirens spilled into the store as police cruisers pulled up in front of the building. Anita looked up and saw the flashing lights of the police vehicles through the front windows. Tameka was still frozen in place and looked back at Anita who had tears streaming down her face.

"Bye Tameka," Anita said as she held the gun to her head and pulled the trigger as Tameka screamed no.

Anita's body fell backwards and her gun slid across the floor as she impacted the hard surface. Tameka crumbled to her knees and threw up all over the floor as police officers rushed in and checked both bodies to find no pulse for either woman. Everyone in the store quickly spilled outside and some had to be told that it was safe to leave the walk-in freezer in the back of the store.

Paramedics soon rushed in and determined that there was no hope for either woman to be revived as they both suffered mortal wounds. Tameka was extremely shaken and had to be assisted by a paramedic in order for her to walk out of the store. As the building was roped off with yellow crime scene tape a police detective came up to Tameka. The detective asked Tameka who she was, what she saw and if she knew the two women.

"I knew both of them. We all went to high school together," Tameka said.

"Did you talk to either of them before the shooting?" detective Stafford asked.

"I talked to Anita before it happened. We hadn't seen each other in a long time," Tameka said.

"Anita, that's the name of the woman that did the shooting, right?" Stafford asked.

"Yes," Tameka said.

"Did she say anything that would be a reason she did this?" Stafford said.

"She said she caught Keisha having sex with her husband," Tameka said.

"Wow. Did she say anything else that sounded odd?" Stafford said.

"Yeah, she did. I asked her if she said anything to her husband about it and she said no, they didn't know that she knew what was going on, but they would soon," Tameka said.

"Then she walked up and shot her?" Stafford asked.

"Yeah, we were standing in the checkout line when Anita just walked up and shot her. Then she shot herself. I still can't believe it," Tameka said with a distant look in her eyes.

"Okay, Miss Davis. Thank you," Stafford said.

Just then Tameka saw her mother and father drive up. Tameka called them and said she didn't think she could drive home after what happened. Tameka's father drove her car back home with Tameka in the passenger seat and her mother followed with the children in the back. Gregory Davis drove Tameka over to her house so she could get out of her bloody clothes and take a shower. The last thing Tameka wanted was for her children to see the blood stains on her clothes. Once they went inside her house Tameka collapsed into her father's arms crying.

"Daddy, it was just awful? Anita just shot Keisha in the head right in front of my eyes. Her blood flew all over the place. Then while I was looking at her, Anita pulled the trigger again and killed herself," Tameka said while sobbing.

"I know baby, I know. It'll be all right," Gregory said as he patted Tameka on her back.

"Daddy, I'm sorry, but I've never seen anything like that," Tameka said.

"You're not supposed to see things like that. That kind of stuff should only happen in war, not in a grocery store. You can cry on my shoulder anytime you want. You're still my baby girl," Gregory said.

"Thanks daddy," Tameka said as her father kissed her on the forehead.

"I'll be out here raiding your refrigerator while you get cleaned up. Then well go over to the house," Gregory said.

"Okay daddy, just don't eat the banana pudding mama made for me. I'll be back out soon," Tameka said.

Tamika removed her clothing that was still splattered with Keisha's blood and turned the water on in her shower while she stood naked in her bathroom with tears streaming down her face, Tameka stepped into the shower and felt the water wash over her body. When the water cascaded over Tameka's head she looked down and saw the red tinted liquid circle the drain around her feet as Keisha's remaining blood washed from her hair. Tameka felt the shower left her physically clean, but still emotionally scarred. After about thirty minutes Tameka came into the kitchen.

"Daddy, put that spoon down," Tameka said.

"I just took one spoonful of banana pudding. You know how good it is after it been sitting in the refrigerator for a couple of days. I called your mama and she's making you a fresh bowl right now," Gregory said.

"In that case, let's finish this off before we leave," Tameka said as she got a spoon out of the drawer.

Once again the father and daughter shared moments bonding together eating their favorite dessert like they did when Tameka was a little girl.

"Tameka, I think you need to take a few days off. You're not going to be able to concentrate on work after seeing something like that," Tameka's mother, Sonya, said after she was at her parent's house.

"I know, but I'm already taking time off when Datron comes down here in a few weeks. I've got some personal days. I'll take the rest of the week off. I still can't believe Anita did that, it sends chills down my spine whenever I think about it," Tameka said.

"Let's talk about something else. This Datron that's coming down to see you, what's that all about?" Sonya asked.

"He's a friend of Lindsay's husband and I talked to him when I went to Oklahoma. He remembered me from Lindsay's wedding and was asking about me," Tameka said.

"Did he play football with Lindsay's husband?" Sonya asked.

"They did play together and became good friends. Datron was RJ's best man at Lindsay's weapon," Tameka said.

"That great big guy?" Sonya asked.

74

"Yes mama, the great big guy," Tameka said.

"Good lord. I wouldn't want all of that on top of me," Sonya said.

"Mama! I can't believe you said that. You're a mess. He's a nice guy," Tameka said laughing.

"What are ya'll talking about in there?" Gregory asked from the kitchen table.

"You don't need to hear this. Keep your nose out of our conversation," Sonya said.

"Sonya if you said I don't need to hear it, then I don't need to hear it. Tameka there's no telling what your mama will say. Tasha, put that cookie down little girl or grandpa is going to get you. It's too late to be eating that. Look at that she's eating it anyway and looking at me out of one eye," Gregory said.

"Good lord, him and those kids of yours. Tell me about this Datron, why was he up in Oklahoma talking about you? He only saw you one time," Sonya said.

"I guess he liked what he saw? Lindsay said that he couldn't get me out of his mind," Tameka said.

"What part of you couldn't he get out of his mind?" Sonya asked.

"Okay mama, she said he liked the way my bridesmaid dress hung off my behind," Tameka said.

"Umhum, I'll bet he liked that. You got that high behind from your daddy's side of the family. Men now days always talking about a woman donkey butt and all of that mess," Sonya said.

75

"Mama, how do you know about that kind of stuff?" Tameka asked.

"I've got satellite television. I watch that reality show where one of those women is always talking about her donkey butt. It's just ridiculous. That donkey butt of yours helped you get those three kids in there. Is this Datron a serious man?" Sonya asked.

"Yes mama he's a serious guy. A woman that he married did him pretty dirty and he's a little scared of moving too fast," Tameka said.

"That's not all bad. In relationships, just like in driving, speed kills," Sonya said.

"Mama, I need to get these kids and go home. It's getting late," Tameka said.

"Are you sure you don't want to stay here tonight?" Sonya asked.

"No, I'll be okay, but thanks," Tameka said.

Tameka took her children, went home and put them in bed. After the children were asleep, Tameka sat in the living room and felt the emptiness until her cell phone rang.

"Hey Lindsay, thanks for calling me back. You won't believe what happened," Tameka said.

"What is it?" Lindsay asked.

"I was in the grocery store and ran into Anita Smith, you remember from high school. Yeah, the light skinned girl. Well, I started talking to her and asked how her husband Montel was doing. She told me that she caught him messing with Keisha," Tameka said.

"What, they've been together since high school. Is Keisha just screwing everybody's man, can't she get one of her own?" Lindsay said.

"Lindsay, Keisha's dead. Anita shot her right in front of me in the grocery store and then she told me bye and shot herself in the head. It was awful," Tameka said.

"What?! Are you fucking kidding me?! That's horrible, are you okay?!" Lindsay asked.

"I can still see it in my mind just as clear as when it happened, but I'll be okay with time. It's just not something that anybody should ever have to see," Tameka said.

"I'm coming down there in the morning," Lindsay said.

"No Lindsay, you don't have to do that. I'll be fine," Tameka said.

"Are you sure?" Lindsay said.

"Yeah, I'm sure. I'm taking a few days off," Tameka said.

"Okay, Tameka you take care of yourself sweetie. I love you," Lindsay said.

"I love you too Lindsay. Bye," Tameka said.

Tameka took off the next day and was relaxing on her sofa about two o'clock in the afternoon when her doorbell rang. Tameka was puzzled, but she answered the door and was shocked.

"What the hell are you two guys doing here?!" Tameka said in surprise.

"I heard about what happened and had to come see you," Datron said as he hugged Tameka.

"I'm hard headed and came even when you told me not to," Lindsay said.

"Now you got me crying. I can't believe that you're here. Where's RJ" Tameka said as they sat down.

"He couldn't get away so he stayed home with the kids," Lindsay said.

"So, Datron, you drove all the way down here with Lindsay. Did she ever stop talking?" Tameka asked.

"You know, she does talk a lot, but she went to sleep after we stopped and ate. Then she snored," Datron said.

"Datron! I didn't talk that much and I don't snore," Lindsay said.

"Yes, you do snore, but you'll never admit it," Tameka said as Lindsay stuck her tongue out at her.

"She had me driving by your old high school and showed me some old club you guys used to sneak off to. I think I know about everybody you went to high school with," Datron said.

"Datron, I just wanted to fill you in on the local history," Lindsay said.

"And RJ, oh my God! Datron, be careful, don't speed. That's my baby you got in your car. What have you done to that man Lindsay?" Datron said.

"RJ said all that?" Tameka said.

"Datron, don't you worry about what I've done to RJ. You need to concentrate on what Tameka could do to you," Lindsay said.

"Lindsay! Don't you go around saying stuff like that? Me and Datron are just getting to know each other better," Tameka said.

"How are you feeling? I mean, it sounded crazy to be caught up in something like that," Datron remarked.

"I'm doing okay. I just can't believe Anita shot Keisha like that. I didn't like Keisha because of what she did to me, but to actually kill somebody over a man, never. A grown person has their own free will and if he decided to get involved with another woman he did that on his own, the woman didn't force him," Tameka said.

"That's how I felt when my ex-wife cheated on me, as much as I loved her, she made that decision. What if I had gone over and killed the guy, then I'm in prison and she's gone anyway. It makes no sense," Datron said.

"Well how long do you guys plan to be down here?" Tameka said.

"Well we have to get back tomorrow night, so we'll leave about three so we can miss the Dallas rush hour traffic on our way back," Lindsay said.

"I've got a hotel room and Lindsay said she was staying with you. I told her that she should at least ask you first," Datron said.

"Lindsay doesn't have to ask. She's like my sister," Tameka said.

"I don't see women with that kind of friendship too often. That's good. I'm still coming back down in a few weeks so we can spend some time together," Datron said.

"Okay, I'm looking forward to it. My mom wants you to come over for dinner when you come back," Tameka said.

"Your mother taught both of you to cook, right?" Datron asked.

"Yes she did," Lindsay said.

"That's what I'm talking about. I'm losing weight, but I still like to eat," Datron said.

Although Tameka told Lindsay that she didn't have to come and check on her, it lifted Tameka's spirits to no end to see her best friend and seeing Datron was an added bonus, because his presence in her home made their relationship real.

The next day came and the time for Lindsay and Datron to go back to Oklahoma had slipped up on them. They all stood in Tameka's front yard saying their goodbyes. Datron and Lindsay were sitting in his vehicle with the motor running when Datron suddenly got out and walked up to Tameka who was standing in her front yard so she could watch them drive off. Datron took Tameka in his arms and kissed her as deeply as he could and she wrapped her arms around his neck and kissed him back. Datron then got back into the driver's seat and drove off.

"Damn Datron, look at you! You're giving Tameka something to remember until you get back, huh?" Lindsay said.

"You know what, you wild, but I can see why RJ is crazy about you. I think Tameka is a good woman and you're a good friend," Datron said.

"You're just a big old teddy bear aren't you Datron?" Lindsay said with a laugh and pinched his cheek.

"Stop that. You're something else. Don't tell any of the other fellas I'm a teddy bear, because I've still got my bluff in on them," Datron said with a laugh.

8

Tameka decided that she would not attend the funerals of Anita or Keisha because it would be too emotionally painful. In a sad coincidence Anita and Keisha's bodies were in the same funeral home but in different viewing areas. Tameka visited and viewed both bodies and wrote her name in the visitor's book of both women since she was the last person to see both of them alive. After the services were complete, Tameka felt she could move past that sad chapter in her life and look forward to Datron's visit. Datron's parting kiss left her with some eagerness to see him again, but she was uncertain of how things would develop, because she had really only been with him twice for any length of time.

Datron arrived in town and came over to visit Tameka after her children had gone to school.

"Well, we're here. What do you want to do?" Tameka asked.

"I just want to sit here and talk about life. What you like to do and how you feel about men, relationships and what you want out of life," Datron said.

"I'm glad to hear you say that, because sometimes when people go out in public, they are kind of putting on a front and trying to impress each other. That's for show. I want to know the real Datron," Tameka said.

Datron and Tameka talked for hours about their lives, families and how they arrived at where they were in life.

"I'm starting to get hungry. Do you want to go get something to eat?" Datron asked.

"No. I'll cook something," Tameka said.

"You're going to cook something?" Datron said.

"Yeah, it won't take long. Do you like fried chicken, creamed corn and green beans?" Tameka asked.

"Now you're talking. How do you keep your figure eating like that?" Datron asked.

"I don't eat that stuff all the time. I cook a lot of baked foods now, but every so often I like to go back to my old favorites," Tameka said.

Tameka began to cook and unexpectedly she had a helper in the kitchen as Datron pitched in to assist.

"Oh my goodness. This is delicious. You can really cook," Datron said.

"What do you want to drink? I've got water, juice, soda and Kool-Aide®," Tameka said.

"What flavor of Kool-Aide®, do you have red?" Datron asked.

"Datron, red is not a flavor, but I have cherry flavor," Tameka said.

"That's what I'll have," Datron said.

After their meal, Datron and Tameka sat down and snuggled on the sofa.

"You know I really don't have men over at my house. I never have, but now all of my children are old enough to be in school now. So you're here with me. It occurred to me that my 'no men at the house rule' didn't stop me from having two more children after my first one. I guess it wasn't where the men were that mattered, but the decisions I made when I was with them that counted," Tameka said.

"Yeah, but your daughter is like five years old now, so it seems like you started making better decisions. You didn't have any more children outside of marriage after her," Datron said.

"When I threw my ex-husband out, he told me that no other man would want me with three kids except as a side piece. Was he right?" Tameka asked.

"Your ex-husband was an idiot. You judge people on their heart, not their past. You have a good heart," Datron said.

Tameka looked at Datron, rubbed his cheek and kissed him.

"Datron, that's so sweet," Tameka said as she snuggled up to Datron again.

"You know, I would like to take you out somewhere on Friday night. Do you think your mother will keep the children?" Datron said.

"Of course she will. She loves to spoil them," Tameka said.

Datron left and went to his hotel room and Tameka kissed him as he left.

On Friday night Tameka took her children over to her mother's house to spend the night. Datron picked Tameka up and they went out to dinner in Tyler. Later the pair went to a club for a little dancing and relaxation.

"Datron you're pretty smooth on the dance floor," Tameka said.

"I do okay. I've got that smooth big man glide," Datron said.

Tameka was wearing a dress that came down to her ankles with a thigh high split and it fit snuggly on Tameka's trim body. As Datron danced with his hands in the air, Tameka would turn her back to him and he kept his eyes on the object that first captured his attention, Tameka's fabulously sculptured ass. Right before midnight, Datron and Tameka left the club and started on the thirty minute drive back to her house. Once they arrived, Datron walked Tameka to her door and they kissed. Datron looked Tameka in the eyes. Tameka opened the door, took Datron's hand and led him inside.

Datron kissed Tameka and she paused as if in debate about whether she could continue given the poor judgment she showed with Braeland, but this was not a boy like Braeland, but a real man. Sitting on the sofa, Tameka kissed Datron back and he began to unzip her dress and pulled it down to her waist. Tameka unfastened her bra and then she felt Datron's large hands on her breasts. Datron then placed gentle kisses on one of the most sensitive areas of her body. Datron's mouth seemed to entirely engulf one of Tameka's breasts while she held the back of his head in her hands.

Tameka's breathing was becoming more rapid in nature as she unbuttoned Datron's shirt and felt the massive chest of this man that felt like he was made of solid muscle. Datron picked Tameka up like she was weightless and carried her to the bedroom. No other man had been in Tameka's bedroom since she had split with her husband.

Datron placed Tameka on the bed and finished removing her dress and he kissed her bare stomach. Tameka kept her figure trim, but after three children she did have a few stretch marks on her abdomen that she was somewhat self-conscious about, but Datron kissed each one lovingly. Datron stood, removed his pants and turned to Tameka. Datron still had his underwear on and Tameka was naked except for her panties. Datron lay alongside Tameka and they kissed and caressed each other tenderly until Datron slipped his hand under the waistband of Tameka's black panties and slowly pushed them down. Tameka removed her underwear the rest of the way and kicked them off her feet. Tameka then watched as Datron removed his boxers and gasped at the sight she beheld. Datron was a big man in every way.

Datron climbed onto the bed and kissed Tameka in a new location where she wasn't expecting that kind of attention, but she wasn't about to tell him to stop. Tameka found herself thrusting her hips upwards because Datron was hitting all of the right spots. Datron then crawled up Tameka's body until he was looking her in the eyes. Tameka kissed Datron and tasted her own essence on his lips. Tameka then felt Datron's presence beckoning for access to her feminine treasure and he had prepared her well to receive him. Tameka eyes widened as she accepted this man. Datron made his entrance into her center and Tameka accepted him. Tameka adjusted her body to accommodate the size of his physical girth, but found she was able to hook her legs into the bend of his his arms and relinquish control to Datron.

"Oh Datron, baby. A little bit more, that's it. Oh yes, baby," Tameka said.

Datron paused as he kissed Tameka deeply and stroked her hair that was a shoulder length weave. Datron then began to withdraw and came back with force until he made contact with Tameka's body. Tameka felt the power contained in Datron's body and he was unlike any man she had been with. Soon Datron was literarily lifting Tameka's body off the bed with his movement and she was meeting him motion for motion with her arms locked around his massive neck.

"That's it baby. Oh yes. That's so good!" Tameka said.

"Yes, Tameka, I've been thinking about this since the day I first saw you," Datron said.

"Is that pussy good to you baby?" Tameka asked.

"Yes it's good, but turn that ass over so I can see it," Datron said.

Datron sat up and Tameka got on her hands and knees.

"That's what I'm talking about," Datron said as her entered Tameka from behind.

"Oh shit Datron, you're in me so deep!" Tameka said.

Datron rubbed his hands across Tameka's ass he moved behind her. Tameka was worked up into a torrid state and was almost slamming her rear into Datron solid mass of a body.

"Oh shit! Oh shit, I'm coming!" Tameka said as she shook, trembled and ground her pelvis against Datron.

"Oh fuck!" Datron said as he exploded.

Afterwards they lay on the bed, looked at each other and laughed.

"Damn Datron! Where did all of that come from? You were Mr. Quiet until we got in bed and you came out of your shell," Tameka said.

"Well, I've been thinking about this for a long time. I guess I got a little excited, but it was even better than I imagined it would be," Datron said.

"So you've been thinking about me. That's sweet. Let me give you something else to think about," Tameka said as she slipped downward in the bed.

"What are you doing? Oh yeah, I see what you're doing now. Oh, that feels so good," Datron said.

Tameka was in charge this time as she brought both Datron and herself to their pinnacles of pleasure once more.

"Tameka, I hate to leave and go to that hotel room. Datron said as they stood in the living room kissing. You're one hell of a woman. Why don't we take the kids to the zoo or something tomorrow?" Datron said.

"Datron, I don't know. I've never really brought men around my children until I was married. I don't want to confuse them. What if you just disappear…" Tameka said.

Before Tameka could finish speaking Datron silenced Tameka by kissing her and rubbing his hands all over her body. Tameka was getting heated up again.

"I'm not going anywhere," Datron said.

"Sure, we can take the kids to the zoo in Tyler. Just call me. Bye Datron," Tameka said breathlessly as Datron walked out of the door.

Tameka sat down on the sofa and just smiled.

The next day Datron called and said he was coming by to take everyone to the zoo and the children were very excited. Tameka was very apprehensive because she broke a rule that she had held for a long time to not expose her children to any man she was not married to, but then she remembered what happened with Terrance when he never really spent time with her children before they got married. Tameka thought that maybe it was a good thing for Datron to want to spend time with her children and not just her alone.

"Okay kids, you remember Mr. Jenkins, from Aunt Lindsay's house in Oklahoma. We'll he and mama are friends and we're all going to the zoo today. Won't that be fun?" Tameka asked.

"Why did you come down here from Oklahoma?" Joquan asked.

"He came to see me and needed to talk to me about something," Tameka said.

"Are you going to come live with us like Terrance did?" Malik asked.

"No, Mr. Jenkins is not coming to live with us. We're just going to the zoo to have some fun. I want all of you to go inside and use the bathroom one more time before we leave," Tameka said as she looked at Datron.

All three children ran inside the house.

"Tameka, I'm sorry. I guess I wasn't thinking. I've never..." Datron said.

"You've never dated a woman with children before. Well, maybe that's where I made a mistake with Terrance. I almost hid my children from him until it was time for us to get married. He knew them, but he didn't really know what it was like to have three kids around all the time until after he moved in and he couldn't handle it. So, if you're going to be with me, why not get the whole experience. It's not all hot sex like last night you know," Tameka said.

"Well hey, I know that. You don't hold back and tell it like it is, don't you? I like that," Datron said.

"I got that from my mother," Tameka said.

Datron took Tameka and her children to the zoo and he had a great time. The experience of multiple stops for bathroom breaks, eating lunch with three children at the table and even loading his vehicle with two car seats was an eye opener for Datron. Instead of going back to Tameka's house they stopped at her parents so Datron could meet them. Tameka's parents were impressed by Datron and thought he was a good man overall, but they were not sure of his long term intentions.

Datron's visit was coming to an end and he and Tameka had spent most of every day together for a week. It was a Monday morning and the children were in school and Tameka was going back to work the next day. Datron had checked out of his hotel room and stopped at Tameka's house before he left.

"Well, I guess this is goodbye," Tameka said.

"Yeah, I guess so. I had a good time with you and your kids," Datron said.

"They didn't scare you off did they?" Tameka asked.

"Naw, I already knew you had three children. They're good kids because you raised them right. Lindsay told me that when I first asked about you, but you were with someone and then you got married. I'm sorry your marriage didn't work out, but if it hadn't, I wouldn't be here right now. I hate to leave," Datron said.

"Well don't leave just yet," Tameka said as she kissed Datron and led him into the bedroom.

Tameka made sure she gave Datron something that would make him eager to see her again.

"Tameka, I want you and the children to come visit me at my home, maybe during spring break or something when the kids have some time off. I want to see where this is going because I have strong feelings for you, but you have to see me in my world too. I'm going to miss you," Datron said.

"I'm going to miss you too," Tameka said wiping a tear.

Datron went back to Oklahoma and Tameka went back to work. Tameka's outlook on life was decided better than it was before and even running into Braeland at work did nothing to dampen her mood. Tameka was sitting in her office when her cell phone rang.

"Lindsay, what's up?" Tameka asked.

"Datron is almost skipping around up here. What happened? You didn't even call and tell me," Lindsay said.

"Nothing much, but we had a good time," Tameka said.

"Good time. You gave him some, didn't you?" Lindsay asked.

"I'm not talking about that, even if I did," Tameka said.

"You don't have to say anything. I can hear it in your voice. You put that good good on his ass didn't you. Work that shit girl. He must have liked it because it was Tameka this and Tameka that, when he came over the other day. I heard him tell RJ that he really likes you," Lindsay said.

"Really! Well, I'm coming up to see him with the kids during spring break. He said he wanted me to see his house and how he lived," Tameka said.

"He's trying to reel you in. When a man wants you to see how he lives, he's really saying, this is how you could be living if you're with me. I'm excited. I knew you were going to put it on his ass when he got down there, good job," Lindsay said.

"Lindsay, you made it sound like I was trying to screw my way into his heart or something. I'm not a hooker," Tameka said.

"You can call it whatever you want to, but that old saying about the way to a man's heart is through is stomach is bullshit. They way to a man's heart is working on that thing below his stomach, if you know what I mean. If you do that shit right you don't have to know how to boil water and he'll still kiss your ass, but if you can cook in the kitchen and the bedroom, his ass ain't going anywhere," Lindsay said.

"I hear you, but I guess that wasn't enough for Terrance," Tameka said.

"Well remember I said a man, not an overgrown boy because that's all Terrnce was. You said his ass has been struggling since you kicked him out. Some people don't know a good thing when they have it," Lindsay said.

"I guess you're right. I've got to get back to work. It was good to hear from you. Love you," Tameka said.

"Love you too girl, you get that man, put it on his ass again until he taps out," Lindsay said.

"You are so crazy, bye," Tameka said.

Tameka was feeling good about her relationship with Datron and the direction her life was headed in general. A department manager slot opened up at her office and Tameka applied and got the position. Tameka was now Braeland's manager's boss, so in effect, Braeland worked for her now.

Spring break arrived and Tameka drove to Oklahoma City with her children to spend a few days with Datron. Tameka arrived at Datron's home and was amazed at the size of his house. Seeing Datron's place reminded her that he retired with an excellent chance to be enshrined in the Pro Football Legend's Hall along with his friend RJ Jefferson, after all Datron opened many of those holes that RJ ran through to gain his yards when he was playing.

"Welcome to my home. Hey kids. Everybody, come on in," Datron said as he kissed Tameka on the cheek.

"This is so nice," Tameka said.

"Let me show you where everybody will sleep. I've got plenty of room," Datron said.

Datron directed everyone to a room of their own to sleep in, including Tameka. Tameka's room was on the bottom floor along with the master bedroom that Datron slept in. Datron gave Tameka the grand tour while the children occupied themselves in his game room. When they were touring the upstairs section of the house, Datron pulled Tameka into a room and kissed her.

"I've missed you and am so glad you're here," Datron said as he kissed Tameka again.

"I've missed you too. I feel something else that tells me that you've really missed me. We'll have to take care of that later," Tameka said.

"That sounds good to me," Datron said.

"I guess we had better get downstairs. I hear Tasha telling Malik to stop doing something to her. They're always getting into it over one thing or another," Tameka said.

"That's the way my older brother used to do me, until I got bigger than he was, and then he left me alone," Datron said.

"Hey, are you guys hungry?" Braeland asked.

"Yes!" all three kids said in unison.

"Why don't we go to this pizza place in town where they have games and a bowling alley?" Datron said as the children screamed in agreement.

After they arrived at the pizza restaurant and ordered food, Datron began to teach the children how to bowl. Datron was quite good at bowling. Tameka watched Datron interacting with her children and saw this man for the first time in a new light as a potential mate and leader of her family. Tameka tried to suppress those thoughts because of how things turned out with Terrance who had left a deep scar on her psyche.

"Mama, did you see me, I got a strike?" Joquan said proudly.

"I saw that, good job," Tameka said as she high fived her son.

"Mama, I need to use the bathroom," Tasha said as Tameka took her by the hand.

Datron drove over to RJ's house to visit with their friends. RJ and Datron sat in the den and talked while Lindsay caught up with Tameka.

"Datron what are you going to do? It looks like things are going well with Tameka," RJ said.

"Things are going well. I'm crazy about her. I feel a certain way, but I don't want to move too fast. It would be a big change for me," Datron said.

"Yeah, it would be a big change. I went through that same change and it was the best thing that ever happened to me. Now I've got a reason to get up in the morning. We went down a similar path with our ex-wives and Lindsay helped put me back together again. I think Tameka is that same kind of no bullshit woman. They went through hell together, made mistakes and they still held their heads up high and took care of the important things," RJ said.

"It's good to see you. How are things?" Lindsay asked Tameka.

"Well when we were out today, Datron spent a lot of time with the kids at the bowling alley and he was great. I saw him differently, you know as a potential father and husband. I thought I was crazy for thinking about that," Tameka said.

"Why is that crazy? That's the way you should be looking at a man, unless you're some woman just looking for a good time. You have allowed Datron to get close to your children, you've never done that before this early in a relationship," Lindsay said.

"I know and it's scaring me, because I'm feeling something for him. It's going on a year now, but we have just not been together much because of distance, at this rate will we ever know if this is going anywhere?" Tameka said.

Lindsay just gave Tameka an exasperated look and a hug.

"Hey let's go see what the guys are up to," Lindsay said.

Once back at Datron's house the children were worn out from playing with their friends and quickly went to bed. Datron and Tameka sat in the den talking.

"Tameka, I need to tell you something. I know this has been a strange situation with us in different places, but being with you has made me realize something. A man is not supposed to be alone in life and you make me happy. I don't want to make a mistake and lose you because of our situation. This is going to sound strange," Datron said as he pulled a box out of his pocket and got down on one knee.

"Datron what are you doing?" Tameka said with a tremble in her voice.

"Tameka, I know I want to be with you. I also know we haven't spent a lot of time together, but you know what, I know what my heart tells me and I understand we still need time to learn more about each other. I want you to be my wife, I love you. Will you marry me," Datron said as he produced a ring with a large diamond.

"Oh my God, Datron. I didn't expect this. Yes, I mean, I want to say yes, but it seems so soon. I don't know what I'm saying," Tameka said as she kissed Datron.

Tameka put the ring on her finger and looked at it. It felt surreal.

"Datron, I'm still shocked. When did you plan this?" Tameka said.

"I've been thinking about this for a while since I left your place. I know this seems too fast, but I was struggling with what to do. I didn't want to ask you to be exclusive with me, because I didn't think it was fair with us apart like this. I want to marry you, but I don't know when. Okay, I know I officially sound stupid now. Who gives a woman an engagement ring and says he doesn't know when he wants to get married," Datron said.

"Well my answer is yes. I love you too Datron and I get it. I feel the same way. When I saw you with the kids today, I thought that you looked like you would be a good father, but I tried to keep myself from going there," Tameka said.

"We're engaged now, so let's get that knowing each other better process started," Datron said as he took Tameka's hand and led her to his bedroom.

"Damn Datron, you've really have been waiting on me haven't you. Baby you wrote your name on it tonight," Tameka said.

"That's the way it's supposed to be. By the time you leave, all I want is for you to think of is me when those thoughts cross your mind. If I need to come down there to put out a fire just call me and I'll be there," Datron said.

"Listen to you. Since you put a ring on it you've started talking a little smack. I like it," Tameka said.

"Well, you know when you first meet somebody you try to be a little cautious and not make a mistake, now that we know each other better we can relax a little. You know what I want now?" Datron said.

"What's that? Tameka asked.

"I want to see my favorite ass, back that thang up here girl," Datron said.

"Datron, come on and get it baby," Tameka said as she got on her knees with her rear in the air.

"Lord, have mercy," Datron said.

"That's it baby, go deep," Tameka said as they engaged once again.

The next day Tameka was over talking to Lindsay when she spotted her ring.

"What the hell is that? That's an engagement ring! Datron proposed?!" Lindsay asked.

"Yes, Datron proposed, but we don't know when we're getting married," Tameka said.

"What do you mean?" Lindsay said.

"We really don't know each other that well, but he said he didn't want to lose me and that he wanted me to be his wife, so he proposed as a stronger commitment, but we're not planning a wedding yet. I totally understand where he was coming from, because I'm not ready to get married real soon myself, but it's nice to know that's where we're headed," Tameka said.

"Was it romantic?" Lindsay said.

"Well it wasn't like your proposal on national television in a football stadium, but it was nice. I was actually shocked. I was thinking, this man has lost his mind, but when he said things the way he did, it was romantic, because it was a grown up way to do it. We've both been crapped on by someone during our first marriages, so taking it slow makes sense, but I's engaged now?" Tameka said laughing.

"What?" Lindsay said.

"That's from an old movie where a woman tries to impress her father and said, I's married now, never mind," Tameka said.

"So what happened after he gave you the ring?" Lindsay asked.

"I made him tap out," Tameka said.

"That's what I'm talking about. You'll be standing at the altar in no time. Just wait until after you leave, he'll be missing that good good. Look at what happened after he got back from seeing you in east Texas, the next time he saw you, you got a ring. If you did your thing right, he'll give you his whole damn house the next time. If I really want something from RJ, then I break out one of my old stripper outfit from the Secret Garden and put on a full service show and I'm getting what I want. There's nothing wrong with keeping it hot for your man," Lindsay said.

"You're right, nothing's wrong with that at all," Tameka said.

"Congratulations girl. You'll be up here before you know it. Maybe you can help run our centers for girls up here. You've got all the right qualifications," Lindsay said.

"Thanks, if things work out I'll think about that, but I heard that the boss lady is a real bitch," Tameka said.

"I'm gonna get your ass for that. That was a good one. I'll see you later," Lindsay said laughing as Tameka left.

"Yep, let me get back over there before those kids tie Datron up and dump him in the pool," Tameka said.

"Datron what are you doing?" Tameka asked when she got back to his house.

"Making brownies," Datron said.

"Tasha said she wanted some brownies, so I'm making brownies," Datron said.

"Are you going to help?" Datron asked.

"Oh no, I think you got this, but you're going down a bad road," Tameka said.

"What do you mean?" Datron asked.

"She's five. If she figures out that all she has to do is come to you in that little voice and look up at you with those big brown eyes and say I want some brownies and she gets what she wants, you're through," Tameka said.

"Well it works for her mother," Datron said.

"You're getting a lot more than just big eyed looks from her mother," Tameka said laughing.

When Datron's brownies were finished they all sat down and sampled them.

"Datron, these are good. You put black walnuts in them," Tameka said.

"When you live by yourself, you've got to learn how to cook something," Datron said.

"Mama, make Malik stop eating my brownies," Tasha said.

"They're not your brownies," Malik snapped back,

"Hey, hey, cut it out, everybody's sharing the brownies," Tameka said to restore the peace.

It was all too soon before it was time for Tameka to leave and head back home. This time it was really difficult for Tameka and Datron to part after making a commitment to each other. Datron watched as Tameka drove off and disappeared around the corner and his house went from a beehive of activity to silence once again.

Datron and Tameka kept their relationship hot with phone calls and occasional visits. One night Datron was watching television in bed and the incoming text message tone on his cell phone went off. Datron opened the text and a broad smile went across his face as he dialed his phone.

"Tameka, did you just text me a picture of your ass?" Datron said.

"I thought I'd send you something you really liked," Tameka said.

"Man it sure looks good. Goodnight, I love you," Datron said.

"Goodnight, I love you too," Tameka said.

Datron finally crossed over a line and he was where he needed to be. Datron was ready to move their engagement from a wait stage to the plan a wedding phase. Datron called Tameka back and said he wanted to come see her over the weekend and Tameka agreed. Tameka went to dinner with Datron at a local restaurant and when dessert was brought out there was a black box on the tray. Datron took the box and opened it and Tameka saw the largest diamond on a ring that she had ever seen. Datron dropped to one knee and asked Tameka to marry him again.

"Tameka, will you marry me whenever you want your wedding day to be?" Datron asked.

"Yes, Tameka said crying," as Datron removed the first engagement ring and placed the new one on her finger.

Other diners in the restaurant clapped and cheered.

"Isn't that Datron Jenkins who played for Oklahoma?" someone asked.

"Couldn't be, what would he be doing down here?" another man said.

Datron and Tameka were headed for a life together as a family. The reality set in for Tameka that she would be planning another wedding and she hoped this would be the last one. Tameka asked Lindsay to serve as her matron of honor and RJ would repay Datron and be his best man. Tameka and Datron decided that they would make this wedding a small affair for close family and friends.

Tameka set a wedding date in November and that would allow her, Datron and the children to spend their first Christmas together as a family. Tameka felt that for the first time in a while everything was going in a positive direction for her.

10

Tameka came home after her mother insisted that her grandchildren spend the night with her. Tameka would use the time to relax, look through a few bridal magazines and eat some of her favorite ice cream. Tameka relaxed on the sofa, but soon fell asleep until she heard a noise and suddenly woke up. Tameka looked across from the sofa and thought she was dreaming, but then she realized what she saw was real. Sitting across from her, Tameka saw her ex-husband Terrance who was unshaven, unkempt and had a wild look in his eyes.

"Terrance, what the hell are you doing in my house?!" Tameka said in a panic.

"This used to be our house. Come on Tameka, I didn't come here to do anything to you, I just want to talk to you," Terrance said.

"How did you get in here? You need to leave or I'm going to call the police!" Tameka said.

Tameka was terrified and didn't know how Terrance got in her house, his state of mind or what his intentions were.

"Come on Tameka. We were married and loved each other. Look baby, I know I fucked up, please give me another chance. Keisha's gone now, so she won't be a problem this time. I'll prove to you that you can trust me. Tameka, please take me back. I promise I won't let you down again," Terrance said.

"Terrance, what's wrong with you? We've been divorced for over a year now, you need to get out of here and go back to your mother's house," Tameka said.

"Mama kicked me out. She said all I was doing was lying around, playing video games and doing drugs," Terrance said in an agitated voice.

Tameka could tell that Terrance was becoming emotional and she didn't know what he was capable of doing.

"Tameka, I know what's going on with you. You know word gets around in a small town like this. I heard you got a promotion at work and I heard you were getting married again to some big time ex-pro football player like your friend did. That's alright. I guess I'm not good enough for you anymore. A regular nigga like me ain't good enough!" Terrance said as he stood up.

Tameka was getting very frightened because Terrance was becoming very unstable. Tameka had her cell phone lying on the sofa beside her, but she knew if she picked it up Terrance could go off on her. Without making a sudden move, Tameka tapped her phone screen and hit a stored number for her mother's cell phone. When Tameka noticed that the call was answered, Tameka took a calculated risk.

"Terrance you need to get out of my house or I'm calling the police!" Tameka said loudly when she noticed the call was answered.

Tameka's mother heard what was going on, picked up her land line phone and called the police. Tameka moved over until her cell phone was behind her body so Terrance couldn't see it, but her mother's cell phone was still connected and Sonya could hear everything.

"Naw, you and your hoe ass friend decided ya'll had to sell your pussy to some rich niggas. Ya'll ain't nothing but some ratchet hoes. Both of you were broke ass baby mamas, but now ya'll trying to act like some high class bitches. That nigga probably can't even fuck you like I did. I saw him with you around town. That big ass nigga was probably using steroids and can't even get his dick hard anymore. That's perfect for you though, you can sit up in his big house so he can take care of you and your bastard ass kids and you don't even have to fuck him. That's a hell of a deal there," Terrance said as he walked towards Tameka.

"Terrance, stay away from me!" Tameka said.

"Look, you know Keisha's dead now, but that hoe knew how to fuck a nigga right! You were pretty good too, but that nasty hoe would do anything I wanted. Shit, it didn't matter to her. Keisha would take it in every hole. She didn't give a fuck. Since your new nigga ain't gonna be able to give you any hard dick, then you need to get one more taste of this," Terrance said as he pulled his pants down and exposed his erect penis.

"Get away from me," Tameka said as Terrance had positioned his groin right in front of her face.

Tameka then noticed automobile headlights appearing in front of her house through the living room windows.

"Come on bitch! Suck my dick one more time like you use to before we got married. You did that shit good before we got married. You did all kind of freaky shit to me to get my ass, so show me you can still take it all in and if you're good enough, I'll fuck you one more time. That's it, Tameka, come on and suck it," Terrance demanded.

Tameka opened her mouth like she was about to comply with Terrance's request and he closed his eyes in anticipation. Terrance felt Tameka's hot breath on his stiff member.

"Come on bitch, suck it! Ahhhhh! Oh shit! You fucking crazy bitch! You bit me!" Terrance said as he fell over the coffee table holding his penis.

Tameka ran out of the house and into the arms of her father who was standing there with his twelve gauge shotgun in his hands. Gregory Davis was a church deacon, but he was ready to unleash his wrath on Terrance for threatening his daughter.

"Tameka, baby girl are you okay?! Where's that sorry ass nigga?!" Gregory Davis asked.

"Oh my God daddy! I'm fine. He's inside," Tamkea said through tears.

"He's a dead motherfucka!" Gregory said as he started for the house with his loaded shotgun.

Tameka grabbed her father.

"No, daddy please! I don't want you to get into trouble. He's not worth it," Tameka said.

"They won't do anything to me. He broke into your house and tried to hurt you. I'll lay his ass down and the law won't blame me at all for protecting my daughter!" Gregory said.

Just then, a county sheriff's vehicle pulled up and a deputy got out. He knew Gregory Davis.

"Mr. Davis, we got a call. What's going on?" Deputy Scott asked.

"My ex-son-in-law is in there! He broke into my daughter's house and tried to hurt her," Gregory said.

"You alright ma'am?" deputy Scott asked.

"Yeah, I'm okay," Tameka asked.

"Did he have a weapon?" Scott asked.

"No," Tameka said.

"What's his name?" Scott asked.

"Terrance," Tameka answered.

"Terrance, can you hear me?" Scott shouted.

"Yeah, I hear you," Terrance replied from inside.

"Terrance, this is the police. I need you to come out of there with your hands up," Scott said.

Terrance walked out of the house with his hands up over his head and the deputy instructed him to get on the ground with his arms outstretched. Terrance complied and he was handcuffed and led to the squad car.

"That bitch bit me!" Terrance said.

"You're lucky I got here when I did or Mr. Davis would have put that twelve gauge shotgun on your ass and the coroner would be taking you in for cold storage," Scott said.

Deputy Scott took Tameka's statement and transported Terrance to the county jail. Tameka went with her father and spent the night at her parent's house. Tameka called Datron and told him what happened. Datron immediately started his drive from Oklahoma to check on Tameka. Datron arrived at Tameka's parent's home early in the morning and she was thrilled to see him. Datron and Tameka sat under the shade of a tree behind her parent's house.

"Datron, I'm so tired of just one thing or another coming back in my face. It's like I can't escape my past mistakes. From what happened with Keisha to Terrance breaking into my house. It's like I can't just move on with my life. Old women hypocrites at church run me down for having children out of wedlock and my ex-husband has some kind of stalker fixation on me. I can't get away from these people," Keisha said.

"Look, this is a small town. I came from a small town in Mississippi. In small towns people are always in somebody else's business, that's their entertainment. Those women know you have a good job, got your college degree and are probably doing better than their own children. It makes them feel better about their situations to put you down. They know the stuff they are saying about you is bs from years ago. Now, your ex-husband realized how badly he messed up by losing you. He had it all, a smart beautiful working woman that loved him and he threw it away, but it's too late. You're mine now and I'm the luckiest man in the world," Datron said.

"So, I'm yours now Mr. Caveman. Datron, I love you. If we weren't at my parent's house, you'd be getting lucky about right now," Keisha said.

"We could always go over to your place it's not that far," Datron said.

"It's time for my children to get home from school, so welcome to a family of five Datron," Tameka said.

"I can wait," Datron said.

Tameka laughed and planted a kiss on Datron's cheek.

Terrance went on trial one month later and Tameka received a shocking lesson from the criminal justice system. Although Terrance had broken into her home and asked her to perform oral sex on him, the only charge that stuck was one of criminal trespass. Tameka was outraged.

The district attorney explained to Tameka and Datron that since Terrance didn't enter her home with the intent to cause harm to her, he couldn't be charged with the more serious offence of burglary. Tameka was confused, because she thought that burglary meant someone broke in to steal something. The district attorney explained that legally, burglary meant that someone broke in to commit a felony whether it was theft, assault or some other crime. Since the testimony showed that Terrance said he wanted to just talk when he first broke in, it became criminal trespass.

"What about when he asked me to perform oral sex on him," Tameka asked.

"That would have been sexual assault if he had grabbed you and made contact with your mouth with his sex organ by force or threatened you if you didn't do it, but since he just stood there, even though he was close, it didn't qualify," the district attorney said.

"I didn't know what he would do to me if I just tried to get up and leave. You tested him and said he had all kinds of drugs in his system," Tameka said.

"You did the right thing, because he could have easily become violent, it's just how the law works. He actually got the book thrown at him for the charge with a two thousand dollar fine and one hundred and eighty days in jail," the District attorney said.

"How can somebody break into your house, expose themselves to you and just get six months in jail?" Tameka said to Datron as they drove to her house.

"That's crazy. It sounds like unless they really hurt somebody, they might not go to jail at all and just get a fine," Datron said.

"Look, I just need to concentrate on our wedding. Terrance is going to jail. Maybe he'll get all of that garbage out of his system in there. Datron, thank you for coming down here to be with me through this crazy stuff. I wouldn't blame you at all if you ran the other way. Look at all of the insane things that have happened to me since we started seeing each other. I don't want to drag you down with all my baggage," Tameka said.

"Tameka, I love you and I'm not going anywhere. Look, we've got just a few months before our wedding and then you'll move to Oklahoma with me. We can start out fresh, get the kids in school and leave the past behind," Datron said.

"I can't wait, but I will miss my parents. My dad was ready to kill Terrance, he came with his shotgun loaded," Tameka said.

"He sounds like my dad. He's cool most of the time, but he don't play when it comes to his family. As big as I am now, I don't mess with him. You just don't make those old black men mad about some things," Datron said with a smile.

"I could tell he was a pretty serious guy when I met him. He asked me how I ended up with three kids before I was married. I told him I was young and just made some mistakes. Do you know what he said to me?" Tameka said.

"What did he say?" Datron asked.

"He said it sounded like I was just a hard headed young girl and didn't know how to keep my dress tail down. He said it seemed like I had come to my senses and it looked like I would be a better wife to you than that piece of trash you married the first time," Tameka said.

"My dad said that? Damn! He doesn't bite his tongue does he," Datron said.

"I took it as a compliment, I think. He's a good man," Tameka said laughing.

12

Tameka was nearing the final stages of preparing for her wedding and was in the mall in Tyler when she heard someone call her name.

"Tameka," the voice said again.

Tameka turned and there stood Davita Brooks and Vicki Jones.

"Miss Brooks and Miss Jones, what are you two doing here?" Tameka asked.

"We just decided to take a little shopping trip and saw you and decided to say hello. I heard you're getting married soon to an ex-pro football player," Vicki said.

"Yes, I'm marrying Datron Jenkins," Tameka said.

"We're happy for you," Davita said.

"Thank you," Tameka said.

"Tameka, could we sit down and talk to you about something that's been on our minds?" Vicki asked.

"Sure, we can sit over here at this table," Tameka said.

The three women walked over to the table and sat down.

"What do you want to talk to me about?" Tameka asked.

"Well it's about that day in church when you came out of the bathroom and we were standing outside talking. You heard us didn't you?" Davita asked.

"Yeah, I heard every word you said," Tameka admitted.

"We just want to say we're sorry. It was mean and uncalled for. I know what we said was ugly. We're not in a position to be judging anybody. I know I'm not. We've all made mistakes and I have too. One of my mistakes that I thought no one knew about was recently thrown in my face and I thought about what we said about you that day," Vicki admitted.

"Can you forgive two old judgmental fools for being ignorant enough to say what we did and too proud to apologize. Can you forgive us?" Davita asked.

Tameka was stunned by what these two women had to say.

"I can't believe what I'm hearing. The things you said about me that day really cut me to the core. I made mistakes when I was younger, but I've worked hard to do better since then for my kids' sake. Hearing how you felt about me made it seem like it didn't matter what I did for the rest of my life because I would always be judged by my past, but I forgive you because you cared enough to ask," Tameka said.

"Thank you and again, we apologize, but I need to ask you something," Davita said.

"What do you need to ask me?" Tameka quizzed.

"It's about my daughter, Keisha," Davita asked.

"You want to ask me about Keisha. I don't know…" Tameka said.

"Please?" Davita pleaded.

"Okay. What is this about?" Tameka asked.

"I know Keisha was not your favorite person. I know she slept with your ex-husband while you were still married to him and I'm sorry about that, but she was still my daughter. Tameka, you were the last person to see my baby alive, weren't you?" Davita asked.

"Yes, I was the last person to see her alive. I was right there when it happened and I hate thinking about it again," Tameka said.

"I know you do baby. I know you do, but I just need to know one thing. Do you think she suffered or felt any pain?" Davita asked.

"It happened so fast. I don't think Keisha knew what hit her. I never saw her take another breath after, you know. I don't think she had time to feel pain," Tameka said with the images playing in her head again.

Davita dropped her head and squeezed her hands together while Vicki rubbed her back.

"Why did you ask me that?" Tameka said.

"I just had to know. I tried to get Keisha to change her ways. I even told her it was never too late to change her life and used you as an example. I said look at Tameka, she had three kids, no husband and still went back to school and got a college degree. I pointed out that you got a good job and bought your own house, but it just made her angry," Davita said.

"You used me as an example to Keisha? I'm shocked," Tameka admitted.

"I hate to say it, but that's why I think she went after your husband. She didn't understand that just because she could be with another woman's man didn't mean he was with her for the right reasons. It seemed like she craved attention from men and I wondered if it was because her father was never around when she was growing up. I think she wanted to show me that you weren't all that by proving that she could get your husband to be with her. Somehow Keisha thought that proved she was better than you. I loved my daughter, but she was misguided and I apologize for what she did to you," Davita said as she stood to leave.

Tameka grabbed Davita's hand and stood by her.

"I forgave Keisha too. She didn't force my ex-husband to do what he did. No one should have to die like that," Tameka said.

Davita looked at Tameka and hugged her.

"Thank you Tameka. I'm proud of you for not giving up. Take care of yourself and good luck with your marriage," Davita said as she and Vicki left the mall.

Tameka sat back down and held her head in her hands trying to process everything she just heard. Tameka would have never thought that Keisha's mother would hold her up as an example for her daughter to emulate. In some ways getting that unexpected apology and revelation seemed to close the door on two sad episodes in her past.

Tameka then looked at her phone and realized she needed to get to an appointment with the wedding planner to put the finishing touches on her upcoming ceremony.

13

Time marched on and before she knew it, Tameka was about to do something she couldn't imagine all those months ago when she told her ex-husband to leave her home after she caught him cheating on her with another woman. Two days before it was time for Tameka to marry Datron, she and Lindsay were walking down the sidewalk having lunch at a tearoom in the historic downtown area of their hometown.

"Oh, this frozen yogurt is delicious," Lindsay said as she ate a spoonful out of a cup.

"Let's sit over her and finish it before we leave. I can't eat it while I drive," Tameka said.

"That's a good idea," Lindsay acknowledged.

They stopped and sat on a bench in front of the county library.

"I'm surprised you got vanilla," Tameka said.

"You know vanilla is my favorite flavor," Lindsay said with a puzzled look on her face.

"I thought you liked the swirl, you know, the mix of chocolate and vanilla together," Tameka said with a straight face.

"What? Oh, I get it now, the swirl. Very funny Tameka. Asshole," Lindsay said with a smile.

Tameka let out a hearty laugh at Lindsay's response. The two friends were about to get up to go down the steps to get in Tameka's car when two young black men stopped nearby in between two parked cars a few feet away from them and carried on a brief conversation that caught their interest. Tameka and Lindsay listened surreptitiously.

"What up dog?" one of the men asked.

"Just chillin man. What about you?" his friend replied.

"I don't know man. Shit's kind of fucked up right now," the first man said.

"What's up?" the friend asked.

"It's Janika man, my baby mama. She went to court on my ass again. They're garnishing my check. I can barely pay my fucking bills. I ain't got no extra money to do shit. I wanted to go to that concert in Tyler this weekend, but damn, that bitch always sweatin my ass," the first man said.

"That's fucked up, but weren't you already kicking in to take care of your daughter man?" his friend asked.

"Yeah, I was, but we broke up and she's with another nigga now. Why should I pay her when another nigga hittin that pussy?" the first man said.

"It ain't for her, it's to take care of your baby man. If you doing your part, it's up to her to do the right thang with the money," his friend said.

"I know man. I guess I need to get a part time job to take some of this pressure off my ass," the first man said.

"Man you know you were out there fuckin up and that's why she left, don't you?" his friend reminded.

"Nigga, you know I was fuckin up because you were out there fuckin up with me," the first man said.

"I know man, but I'm done with that shit. Me and Remisha got married three weeks ago. We just said, fuck it, went to the court house and did it," the friend informed.

"What?!" the first man said.

"Look we got two kids together already and she put up with all the crazy shit I was doing out there in the streets, other hoes, gettin high and everything else. I was even trappin for a minute. I'm getting too old for that shit and needed to do better for my kids man. It's hard enough out here and without your daddy around, it's worse. My daddy wasn't around for me and I don't want to do that to my kids. Good to see you dog, but I got to get back to the crib man. Stop by sometime and we can slap some bones or something man," the friend said as he got in his car.

The first man watched his friend drive away before dropping his head and leaving in his vehicle.

Tameka and Lindsay looked into each other's eyes and didn't need to say a word. They realized other young women were still walking the same hard road they traveled in the past, but even on that journey there were rays of hope.

Two days later Tameka was sitting in a room in the back of a church with her friend Lindsay and her cousin from Dallas preparing to walk down the aisle to marry Datron Jenkins. The three women stood in a circle, held hands and prayed that Tameka's marriage would be blessed with, love, understanding and longevity.

"Tameka, are you ready?" Lindsay asked her dearest friend.

"Yeah, I'm more than ready. I'm blessed," Tameka replied.

The rest of the wedding party had walked down the aisle and Lindsay was the last person to go before it was time for Tameka to take her final steps as a single woman. Tameka stepped up to the doors to the church and her father was by her side. Datron had not laid eyes on Tameka's wedding dress and he was floored when the wedding march blared out from the organ and the church doors opened. Tameka stepped inside and took three steps inside alone and stopped, Tameka was wearing a designer wedding gown composed of white and royal blue and it hugged her tall lean body before trailing off into a long train. Tameka's makeup was flawless with her long neck, high cheekbones and luscious red lips giving her the presence of an African princess. Her hair was flowing back over her shoulders and cut straight as it stopped at her shoulder blades. Blue and white peep toe pumps with six inch heels finished he ensemble. Gregory Davis stepped in from the back of the church and joined his daughter on the carpet of rice paper. Tameka hooked her arm into her father's arm and they completed their walk up to the front of the church where Datron and the rest of the wedding party were waiting. Gregory placed Tameka's hand into Datron's and took his seat alongside his wife.

The couple said their vows and when Datron got to his part he had a surprise for Tameka. Tameka's mother brought her three children up to the front of the church and they all stood with their mother. Datron read words that he wrote promising to love honor and cherish Tameka and her children and pledged that they are now one family that would stay together forever. It was at this point that Tameka broke form and could not help but start crying, but she brought her emotions under control as the kids took their seats. Datron and Tameka then took each other as husband and wife. Datron kissed his new wife for the first time.

Tameka felt like she had been on a journey alone for ten years and finally she had someone to help her carry a heavy load after a disastrous detour with Terrance. Tameka's best friend, Lindsay, and Datron's best friend, RJ, were smiling almost as much as the newlyweds, because they knew they were good for each other.

As they prepared for the reception, Datron and Tameka looked at each other.

"Datron when I saw you standing alongside RJ at Lindsay's wedding, I would have never dreamed we would end up married, how did this happen?" Tameka said.

"It happened because there was something about you that I just couldn't get out of my head," Datron said.

"What, you mean your favorite body part?" Tameka said.

"Well that caught my interest, but you had this quiet strength about you that caught my attention and I needed to find out where it came from. It comes from your heart and spirit," Datron said as he kissed Tameka.

"Well we need to get out there and do our first dance and then we're going on our honeymoon in Hawaii. I can't wait," Tameka said. After a long night of celebration Datron and Tameka prepared to leave for their honeymoon trip. Tameka said her goodbyes to her children and their new stepfather told them to obey their grandmother who was keeping them during their honeymoon. Tameka and Datron finally boarded their flight in Dallas and took off for Hawaii. For the first time in their relationship, they felt truly alone as a couple.

"Datron, I'm going to enjoy every minute we have together alone as man and wife on our honeymoon. I understand when we get back our life will get busy. I know you love me, you have to, because you are giving up your carefree life and now we are a family of five," Datron said.

"I'm looking forward to starting life with my new family. Maybe we will become a family of six," Datron said while looking at Tameka.

"Datron, do you want to have a baby?" Tameka said.

"I've always thought about it," Datron said.

"I'd be proud to have your child, because I love you," Tameka said.

"We can start practice on making one when we get to Hawaii," Datron said.

Datron previously booked a cabin near the beach, but it was a part of a luxury resort with all of the amenities at their fingertips. On their first night there Tameka wanted to watch the sun set from the beach. The newlyweds sat on beach towels spread out on black sand as the sun disappeared below the horizon.

After the beautiful sunset, Datron took Tameka's hand and they walked back to the cabin. Datron scooped Tameka up in his massive arms, carried her over the threshold and sat her on the bed.

"Did I tell you that you were the most beautiful and sexiest bride I had ever seen? I was standing there to get married, but if I could have, I would have thrown you over my shoulders and ran out of that church with you so we could make love," Datron said as he kissed Tameka.

"You've got me here all to yourself, you don't have to leave and we can wake up together in the morning. You're my husband now. Let me get ready for you. I've got something special that I think you're going to like." Tameka said as she kissed Datron.

Tameka went into the bathroom and fifteen minutes later she walked out with her wedding gown and shoes on. Datron looked at his wife and picked her up and threw her across his shoulder. Datron placed Tameka on the bed and dove under her wedding dress as he knelt on the floor. Tameka couldn't see Datron, but she could feel what he was doing to her underneath her dress as she saw his head moving up and down.

"You're so damn bad, but that feels so good to me," Tameka said.

Datron emerged from underneath Tameka's wedding dress with a big smile on his face. Tameka removed her dress and was soon naked because she wore nothing underneath. Datron stripped down also. Datron began a journey all over his wife's body with his mouth and hands until Tameka was writhing in pleasure. Datron then stood up and did something that no man had ever done to Tameka before. Datron picked Tameka up with his massive arms and held her in the air.

"Tameka, I want you to wrap your body around me and try to get to the other side by going through me," Datron said.

Datron held Tameka in the air with her legs hooked into his folded arms and his hands were on her butt. Tameka wrapped her long legs around Datron's waist and hooked her ankles together. Soon, the couple was intertwined and fully engaged.

"Oh shit Datron. This is so hot," Tameka said.

"That's it baby, just grind on me," Datron said.

Tameka had her arms hooked around Datron's neck and was kissing him the whole time as she ground into his body. Perspiration was soon dripping from their bodies. Datron unfastened Tameka's ankles and was lifting her body in rhythm with his arms.

"Oh, oh, oh!" were the sounds escaping from Tameka's mouth. Before she realized what was happening Datron repositioned Tameka so that she was standing. Datron turned Tameka around and she placed her hands on the bed as he grabbed her ass cheeks and drove into her.

"That's it baby. Oh, oh, oh. Oh fuck!" Tameka said as she climaxed and Datron emitted a groan from deep inside his being and they both collapsed into a heap onto the bed.

"Datron, where did that come from? You were like an animal. I have never been made love to like that before and you can do that to me forever," Tameka said.

"It's been building up inside me. That's the way I've wanted to make love to you for a long time. When I saw you in that wedding dress, something switched on inside me. I said this is my woman, and I'm going to give her everything I've got the next time we make love. I wanted you to feel me inside you and know that what I did was only for you. That's how much I love you. I wanted to consummate our marriage in a way that you would never forget," Datron said.

"I won't forget this for a long time, because you are a man's man Datron and you put something on me tonight that told me that this pussy and my entire body belongs only to you, because nobody has ever did anything to me like you did tonight," Tameka said.

"That's what I'm talking about!" Datron said as he slapped Tameka on her ass.

"You are so crazy," Tameka said laughing.

One thing Tameka made sure they did while in Hawaii was to visit Mt. Kilauea National Park on the suggestion of her friend Lindsay. As they stood on top of the mountain walking on the harden lava flows, Tamkea reflected on her life.

"Datron, this is a harsh place, but even here there are a few plants growing and some have flowers on them," Tameka said.

"You know they say this volcano is still creating new land where the lava flows into the ocean," Datron said.

"I know and sometimes I feel like some of these plants up here. I was in a harsh place during a period of my life and I helped make it that way because of the choices I made, but I survived. Now I want to bloom as your wife and make you happy. I want us to have the best family life ever. Datron, do you know how special you are?" Tameka asked.

"What do you mean?" Datron asked.

"You are changing your whole life for me and my children. You were free to do whatever you wanted to do and go wherever you wanted to go anytime you wanted, but you gave that up for me and my kids. That's amazing to me," Tameka said while looking Datron in his eyes.

"Love is amazing and I love you," Datron said.

Tameka kissed Datron as the howling winds whipped around them.

Datron and Tameka had a fabulous honeymoon. On the night before it was time to fly back to the mainland, Tameka and Datron watched the sun set behind the Pacific Ocean once again as a signal that one chapter of their lives together was ending and another beginning.

Datron and Tameka returned home to the realization that their old lives were gone forever. Tameka and her children moved to Oklahoma City with Datron. Tameka relived memories of when she left Dallas when her children cried at the reality of leaving Lindsay and her kids behind. Tameka's children now wept because they were being separated from their grandparents and friends. The risks of another failed marriage weighed heavy on Tameka's soul and then she felt Datron's reassuring hand on her shoulder.

"Everything is going to be fine," Datron whispered into Tameka's ear as she squeezed his hand.

14

Tameka rented her house in east Texas and accepted a position with RJ and Lindsay's organization to help young men and women get a second chance in life. Later, Tameka became the director of The Lindsay Centers for Young Women when the position became available because the previous director relocated to another city. Everything was going perfect for Datron and Tameka until one night when they came home from dinner

Datron had pulled his vehicle up in the circular driveway. Datron and Tameka had gotten out of the vehicle, but the children were still inside when Datron saw something move in the shadows.

"What was that?" Datron asked.

"What do you mean?" Tameka asked.

"I saw something move by those bushes," Datron said.

A man then stepped out from behind a tree and he was holding a gun.

"Oh my God!" Tameka screamed as the man who was wearing a ski mask stepped forward.

"Hey brother what are you doing here?" Datron asked.

"I'm here to take back what's mine," the man said as he took the ski mask off.

"What! Terrance, no! What are you doing here? Why don't you just leave me alone?!" Tameka screamed.

The children were frozen with fear inside the vehicle.

"Look man, we don't need any trouble here. Why don't you let my family drive on off, then me and you can have a nice talk, okay?" Datron said.

"It's not your family nigga? It's my family!" Terrance said.

"Terrance you need to leave. I'm married, this is my husband. Don't do this!" Tameka pleaded.

"Yeah, I know you're married now. Living up in this big ass house like you a motherfuckin queen. I drove by your hoe ass friend's big house too. She put you up to this shit, didn't she? Probably told you to get rid of me so you can get a rich nigga too. After I'm finished here, that white bitch is next. Ya'll two hoe ass baby mamas who found two dumb, rich motherfuckas and fucked your way in the good life. Motherfucka taking care of your bastard ass kids, every one of them by a different nigga, just so he can get pussy anytime he wants. That pussy worn out anyway after three kids and all them nigga that's been in there. Bitch, I told your ass I had changed, but you had me put in jail. That's it bitch!" Terrance said as he pointed his gun at Tameka.

"Hey man, calm down! You don't want to do this," Datron said.

"Shut the fuck up, nigga! Look at me now. This was my wife and my family! She used to fuck me and suck my dick! Now, I ain't got shit! If I can't have her then ain't nobody gone have her!" Terrance said as he leveled the gun at Tameka and pulled the trigger.

The gun fired, but Tameka was still standing because Datron still had his football quickness and jumped in front of his wife by the time Terrance pulled the trigger, Datron went down in a heap on the ground. Terrance took off running and Tameka screamed as her children cried inside the vehicle.

"Datron! Datron! Oh my God!" Tameka cried as she dialed 911 on her cell phone.

Tameka placed her hand on Datron's chest and it was covered in blood. Datron hadn't moved since he went down and the children were hysterical. Within five minutes the police and an ambulance arrived. Emergency Medical Technicians attended to Datron. Datron was breathing and had a strong pulse. Tameka followed behind the ambulance in Datron's SUV and called Lindsay along the way. Datron was rushed into emergency surgery and Tameka was frantic.

Lindsay arrived and helped calm the children down.

"Tameka, what the hell happened?!" Lindsay asked.

"We came home from dinner and when we pulled up, a man came out of the shadows with a gun. He was wearing a ski mask and then he pulled it off. It was Terrance," Tameka said.

"Terrance, your ex-husband Terrance?" Lindsay asked.

"Yes. He was looking and talking crazy. Datron tried to talk him down and he got loud and started saying all kinds of crazy stuff, then he said if he couldn't have me then no one could. He pointed the gun at me and pulled the trigger. I thought I was dead, but Datron jumped in front of me and saved my life. He's got to make it. The only reason he got shot is because he met me. I'll never forgive myself if doesn't make it," Tameka said between sobs.

"Tameka, what Terrance did was not your fault, he's a grown man, but he's sick and his mind is not allowing him to think straight," Lindsay said.

"My God Lindsay, you should have seen Terrance. He was dirty, unshaven and had a wild look in his eyes. He said the craziest things. He even said he went by your house," Tameka said.

"My house! Why would he go by my house?!" Lindsay asked in a concerned tone of voice.

"He blamed you for me kicking him out and said it was your idea, then he said when he was finished with me, you were next," Tameka informed.

"What?! He's still out there loose. I'm worried about RJ and my kids!" Lindsay said.

"Lindsay, it's okay. The police think he's gone. I told them what Terrance said and they're watching your house, just in case," Tameka said.

"Thanks for telling me. I need to call RJ," Lindsay said.

RJ informed Lindsay that the police filled him in on everything and were watching the house closely. Just then the doctor came out and Tameka rushed up to him.

"Mrs. Jenkins, I've got good news. Your husband is going to be fine. The bullet basically went through the flesh in the pectoral muscle in his chest and caught the fleshy portion of his right arm on the underside on its way out. He can talk if you want to see him," the doctor said.

Tameka walked back to the small room Datron was occupying in the emergency wing of the hospital.

"Datron, oh baby. I'm so happy that you're okay. I'm so sorry this happened. Please forgive me," Tameka said while crying.

"Tameka, why are you apologizing to me?" Datron said slowly as he was still feeling the effects of pain medication.

"If you had never been with me, this would not have happened. You got shot trying to save me. I love you. You were willing to die for me," Tameka said.

"I couldn't lose you. I may as well be dead if you were gone," Datron said as he drifted off to sleep.

Tameka previously provided a statement to the police regarding what happened and supplied a detailed description of Terrance. The shooting of a former professional football player at his home by his new wife's ex-husband made national news, but there was a sad ending to the saga.

A Texas State Trooper stopped behind a car parked along the side of the road on the southbound side of Interstate Highway 35 north of Denton, Texas. The trooper walked up to the driver's side door. When the trooper looked inside the vehicle he saw a man slumped across the middle console with his body stretched across into the passenger front seat with a pool of blood covering the leather seat cushion. The trooper opened the passenger side door discovering a gunshot wound to the man's head and a pistol on the floorboard, it was Terrance. Terrance took his own life when he ran out of fuel on the way back to east Texas as he knew he would be caught eventually and with the pull of a trigger, his downward spiral in life ended in tragedy.

Datron was released from the hospital the next day and went home to recuperate. Tameka and Datron were watching the news when a story about Terrance being found dead alongside the road in Texas was featured. Tameka couldn't believe it. She didn't know how to react, but those emotions came out spontaneously. Tameka curled up to Datron and he held her with his left arm as they lay on the sofa.

"What happened to him? He wasn't even the same person anymore. It's so sad. I'm sorry Datron. I don't care for him the way I do for you, but there's something just not right about how he just lost it," Tameka said as she cried.

The children were in the next room in full view of Datron and Tameka since they were still shaken by witnessing the chaos that unfolded in front of their young eyes.

"Tameka, I understand. You were married to that man and you didn't just stop loving him, he betrayed your trust and you ended the marriage. It seems like he just lost all hope and self respect. As bad as Charmane treated me, I would feel bad if something like that happened to her too. You remember what RJ's ex-wife did after they got divorced? It did a real number on him," Datron said.

"I guess you never know what will happen with someone when things start to go bad for them.

I'm so lucky to have you Datron. I love you," Tameka said as he held her husband.

"I love you to," Datron said.

Datron recovered fully physically and was able to bowl and do everything he could before the shooting. Tameka labeled his bullet scars as love marks since he got them in an attempt to save her life. The family also healed psychologically over time with the help of group counseling sessions that helped them recover from the emotional damage caused by Terrance's actions.

15

Six months after Datron was shot, Tameka and Lindsay were sitting alongside each other in chairs on the deck behind Tameka's home by the pool.

"Tameka can you believed that after all these years, we are sitting here together," Lindsay said.

"It's strange, isn't it? There's something else that brings back memories of the old days, we're both pregnant. Can you believe that?" Tameka said.

"No, I can't. I thought I was through with that, but RJ wanted another kid, I thought he was crazy, but I told him yeah. It feels like when we were younger. It was like one of us was always pregnant," Lindsay said.

"Well, it's a lot different now. We're both married. There're not seven of us living in a cramped apartment in Dallas. We have men that love us that we don't have to chase down to try to get them to help take care of their own children," Tameka said.

"Amen to that," Lindsay said.

"Lindsay, over all of these years what sticks in your mind?" Tameka asked.

"You know, I guess it was when that man called me a thot baby mama stripper when I was dancing at the Secret Garden and I got in that fight with him. He just thought that he had bought me to do anything he pleased just because he paid for a VIP room dance and threw some extra cash on a table. He felt like I was lower than shit on the bottom of his shoe because of what I did to make a living, but it was a just a job to me to put food on the table. I let him know that who I was wasn't defined by his image of me. That's what I remember. What about you?" Lindsay said.

"Mine is what Terrance, God rest his soul, said to me when we split up. He told me that no man would ever want me except as a mistress or side chick because I had three children. He was wrong, because Datron wanted me because he fell in love with me. I wasn't just some baby mama sex target for dogs like that Braeland idiot was talking about that day at my old job," Tameka said.

"You know Tameka, I have a sister, but you're closer to me than she is," Lindsay said as she looked at Tameka.

"Well, I don't have a biological sister, but you are my sister in life," Tameka said as she wiped away a tear.

The two women looked out across the landscape at the open fields behind the home and held hands as they basked in the sun.

About The Author

ESSENCE® bestselling author D.T. Pollard lives in the Dallas/Fort Worth, TX area. He is married and has one son.

Other works
By
D T Pollard
Rooftop Diva – A Novel of Triumph
After Katrina (fiction)
Fools' Heaven – Love, Lust and
Death Beyond the Pulpit (fiction)
TARP TOWN U S A – The
Recession That Saved America
OBAMA GUILTY OF BEING PRESIDENT
WHILE BLACK
Vampire Sapien
The Mark Unmasked
Publish Free For Kindle Today
Sell Worldwide Tomorrow
World Wide Nuclear Power Plant Guide
Unemployed But Not Destroyed
Vulture Capitalism
Whitney Houston – Poems for Whitney
Whitney Amy Michael Elvis
The Good Old Girls Club
President Obama – Diary of Disrespect
Who
Who Moved My Ocean – Avoid The Shrinking Job
Trap

Mitt Romney's America – No Trespassing By The
47%
Romnesia – How Dangerous Is It
Obama 2.0
Carnage Control
Gold Digger's Grave
Things You Can't Tell Mama – The Pastor's Wife
Things You Can't Tell Mama – Her Man Was Once
Yours
Things You Can't Tell Mama – Her Blond Best
Friend
Things You Can't Tell Mama - Mr. Taboo
Things You Can't Tell Mama – The Prophetess
Affair
Things You Can't Tell Mama–Your Best Friend's
Mother
Things You Can't Tell Mama – The President's Sex
Tape
Things You Can't Tell Mama – Anthology
Confessions of a Single Black Woman
Tiberius – Rap's Rainmaker
Things you Can't Tell Mama – The Pastor's Wife 2
Mommy Porn
Jacob's Cabin
The Pastor's Lover
Side Piece
Side Piece 2 – Amber Alarm
Hero In The Hood
The Pastor's Lover 2
She Twerks Hard For The Money
The Pastor's Lover 3
Forget Big Brother We Tell DAD Everything
The Pastor's Wife 3

Hoe Hoe Hoe Merry Christmas
Ghetto Tony and White Trash Tina
Fifty Shades of Plaid
Grandma Does It Better
Keisha's Mama Is So Fine
Less Pretty
Pretty For A Dark Skinned Woman
Massive Monroe
The Pastor's Lover 4 – The Pastor's Wife 4
The Obituary of Gut Bucket Johnson
Forget Big Brother – We Tell DAD Everything
Unreal Housewives of South Dallas
Liquid Memories: You Can Live Forever
Gold Digger's Game
Ebola – Partying With Grace
THOT On The Beach
What Would Dr King Think About Today's Black America
Your Best Friend's Mother 2 – Lust In London
Donald Trump –The Big White Man Returns
Secrets of a Baby Mama

www.ingramcontent.com/pod-product-compliance
Lightning Source LLC
Chambersburg PA
CBHW071311130626
46556CB00004B/1558